RUMBLE BEAR

DEAN HARMAN

 ISBN (Print) 978-1-48359-343-2 (Ebook) 978-1-48359-344-9

I dedicate this book to my nephew
KAI JACKSON,
and my friend and mentor
CHRIS SEARS.

PROLOGUE

A grizzly bear's paw is one of Mother Nature's most remarkable creations; the five hardened black claws are both feared and celebrated by all who live life in the wild. Whether you roam by foot or flight, over sand or through snow, the glimpse of tracks disclosing that a grizzly has wandered over that very spot tells an important story. The size and weight of the tracks we leave in this world quietly tell of the many choices we have made, and they whisper, if only for a few seconds, of the journey we have traveled.

For most creatures, a thick bramble of fear and uncertainty holds them back from feasting on both the sweetness and bitterness of a well-lived life. I can tell you with certainty that almost none of the animals I've encountered in my many seasons have strayed from where they were born. Most haven't even had the courage to venture out into a large circle around their home mountain range or alpine lake. For some unknown reason, when the mystical opportunity to wander presents itself, their spirits drum them home with the promise of a life of comfort and safety. As the years pass, they no longer peer out past the prickly thickets nor dare to wander.

This story is for those special few who have something inside their souls that drives them out into the world, searching for that one path or tiny trail that is meant only for them. It rumbles deep down in their guts—yearning, calling, waiting to be found.

CHAPTER ONE

Life Never Lets You Choose Where It Begins

It was morning. I stared up at the small hole with the shimmering blue lights that seemed to stir all three of us bears. The light grabbed at my mother's hunger. Her long winter fast had depleted her summer energy and burned up most of the fat she had put on last fall.

Those restful days ended as streams of daylight broke the darkness of our hibernation. The light was now too strong to ignore. My sister Tikka and I were nosed into one corner of the den, and my mother, Nahani, began ripping and scraping away at the plug of snow and sticks at our den's tunnel entrance.

"Finally," she grunted and, with a last look in our direction, she squatted and pulled her body out into the sunlight.

Tikka and I breathed in the rush of cool, fresh air. Exciting new smells and limitless curiosity drew my brave sister down the blue canal first. As I poked my head outside our den for the very first time, I remembered just how bright the spring sunlight can be. The snow seemed to amplify the sun's power, and my brand-new eyes felt attacked as if tiny ants with sharpened spears were trying to blind me.

As my vision cleared, I wanted to drink in everything I could see. The best thing I could think to do was to jump. To leap. "Awesome," I yelled, rolling backwards. I found my balance, stood up on my back legs, and looked down the long white southern slope that melted into a variety of greens and browns in the valley below. My imagination purred with the animals and the incredible stories Mother had whispered to us during those long dark weeks in our den.

Tikka nearly ran me over, laughing, jumping, and vibrating with energy. She loved this new playground. She growled and giggled and pulled at my ears. That was my sister, and to this very day she is the most fun-loving grizzly I have ever known.

Tikka had black feet and legs that eventually merged into a rusty brown along her body and head. She was a little smaller than I was, but she was strong, incredibly smart, and, as I found out later, tough.

When I first really saw my Mother in the light of day, she was descending, side-hilling her way back down to the den. Her dark, reedy-brown hair was thick, and a few battle scars on one shoulder gave you the impression she might be quite formidable if she had to be. Her body was long and lean from her deep sleep, and her wise eyes and confident gait made her a truly grand grizzly.

Our last night in the den was tense. Nahani was just too hungry to sleep anymore. Powerful feelings gripped at her mind. Morning light broke and Tikka and I looked up at Mother. Her full attention was on the mouth of the tunnel. She paced, hungry and agitated. "Stay close to me and watch. Listen more than you speak. Do exactly what I say. The world has many dangers, and this first year, your only jobs are to listen, learn, and survive."

The spring seemed to fly by. We traveled to lower elevations where Mother would dig for gophers and grasses. This always seemed to me like a lot of work for just a little meal, but Mother said it was safer for now to eat small and stay in the mountains.

One day, we saw a big male grizzly crossing a river in a valley below us. Immediately, Nahani jumped into action, making us run behind her until Tikka and I were too tired to run anymore.

When the real heat of summer arrived, Mother took us for a treat to a secret place where she said the most delicious things lived and we could have as much as we liked.

For hours we slogged through boulders, shale, and thorns, having no water on the way. "This better be good." I snorted. Mother's famous *be-quiet* stare was soon followed by her *just -try -me* low growl, which silenced me instantly. Just at that very humbling moment, I was tripped by a furry paw, causing me to lose my footing and what was left of my dignity as I tumbled over a rough log. My sneaky, squeaky sister, Tikka, loved to trip me at choice times—always to add a little more sting to an already embarrassing situation.

When the mountain gave way into that lush open bowl, the low green bushes perfumed the air with sweet smells.

Suddenly our steady pace turned into a sprint, and soon we were shoulder-deep in mountain blueberries. We ate berries for a week, and our lips, faces, and paws glowed blue from the juice. I loved the flavor, and I developed a technique so I could eat as many berries as possible as quickly as possible. I rolled my lips over the branches while inhaling, sucking in the mountain's magic berries until I was near delirium.

One afternoon Tikka screamed, "I can't take another berry. One more blueberry and I will run away." This, of course, was the perfect time and place for one of my famous blueberry farts. Her face curled in disgust and, while Mother and I laughed, she waddled away claiming this was grizzly bear abuse. She stayed out of the patch for the rest of the day, but I wasn't done yet. This was heaven! I continued to gorge myself until I was just too full to swallow one more delicious berry.

Tikka and I were growing, and keeping up with Mother was becoming much easier. As the nights grew cooler in the mountains, Nahani said, "We must get more meat if we plan to survive the winter. Great pools of fish called salmon will soon be arriving."

That night when we all curled up together for sleep, Nahani told us a story.

"Mother Nature once told me about a blue grouse named One-Eye that lived with his brothers and sisters in the majestic forest lowlands. As he grew, his mother repeated the three blue grouse rules of life to her children every day. Rule Number One was to never fly more than a few seconds at one time, or else the hawks and eagles will get you. Rule Number Two was that it's always best to stay perfectly still, no matter how close danger may be. Rule Number Three was that nature gave us flight, but she also gave us speed and agility on the ground. The grouse is blessed like no other bird and, if we always follow the rules, we can each have a happy life."

Tikka loved stories. She closed her eyes and sniffed with content as Mother continued.

"Life was pretty easy for One-Eye. He ate the same things and roosted in the same trees almost every day. His favorite time of the day was when he and his family would fly-slash, which was to burst into a low, fast flight. They would travel at blistering speeds over the open terrain, and then dive swiftly back into the timber. Flying was his favorite activity in the entire world. The few seconds of freedom and adventure made him so happy.

"One-Eye's second favorite activity—a distant second—was munching on the scrumptious bright yellow cloudberries that often grew along the small creeks of his home range. He had only ever tasted maybe ten of them, since they grew in high bushes in the direct sun: too open and dangerous a location for him because the quick and cunning raptors were always watching.

"On the first day of fall, One-Eye was feeding on small bugs along a gravel outcrop with his siblings. A shadow flashed and everyone ran into the underbrush, but One-Eye remained perfectly still. Something moved above. He froze, trying to blend in with his surroundings as best he knew how.

"A gentle voice whispered, 'I have always admired your brave ability to stay still in the very face of danger.'

"One-Eye slowly moved just his eyes to peek up into the broad spruce branches right above him. There sat a deadly red-tailed hawk with powerful talons, his huge eyes, peering back at One-Eye.

"'I won't hurt you,' he reassured. 'You see, I only eat rabbit and squirrels. Those are my favorite meals. I would never hurt another bird.

"'I saw you fly over here and I must say, you were quite impressive. Your wing flap speed is very high, but I see that you don't soar or glide much.' The hawk shrugged. 'Well, I guess with hawks like me around, it's not very smart to be gliding very much anyways. But have you ever at least tried soaring?'

"'No…' One-Eye offered.

"'Why not?'

"'Because it's too dangerous. It breaks Rule Number One.'

"The hawk shrugged again. 'Well, would you like to soar high and free and feel the strong winds lift you into the sky?'

"'Yes, I would love that,' One-Eye blurted.

"'Well, what if I fly with you and protect you from anything that might try to harm you? I promise I'll fly below you and not above. If you feel any danger, simply turn and dive into the forest. It will be fine.'

"One-Eye was confused, but he was fascinated by the idea of actually soaring. He finally relaxed, took a deep breath and fluttered up onto the branch beside the red hawk.

"One-Eye looked his new friend over carefully. His eyes were sharp and attentive, and his mighty wings were tucked peacefully away. But those oversize black talons chilled One-Eye's innards.

"The red-tailed hawk turned away and shook out his tail feathers, and in a low, clear voice, masking his hesitancy, One-Eye said, 'Go on then. Launch. I'll follow.'

"Without a word, the hawk sprung lightning-fast off the branch and tore off into the beautiful blue skies above. One-Eye stared for a moment, gazing out past the confines of the forest canopy. The freedom of the bright blue sky was too much. He launched himself, and with a few strong flaps, he gained altitude and broke out into the glorious space above his tiny world.

"In a blink, the hawk was suddenly below and just behind him as they went higher. One-Eye laughed as he looked down at the forests, meadows, and streams beneath. He stretched out his wings in glory. One-Eye held his wings open, caught a warm updraft of wind and then…he soared. He flew like no grouse before him had ever flown. It was glorious and free and absolutely wonderful.

"The red hawk flew closer, and together they enjoyed this moment, this amazing flight. One-Eye dipped his wing to turn and concentrated on the wondrous panorama beneath him. Suddenly, a searing pain shot through One-Eye's body. Merciless talons closed around his neck.

"As the two entangled birds tumbled to earth, One–Eye croaked, 'What are you doing?'

"They plummeted ever faster, the hawk's free talon clawing at One-Eye's head until one talon finally sunk into his eye.

"In agony and confusion, One-Eye pleaded, 'Why are you doing this to me?'

"The remorseless hawk's curt answer was cold and calm. 'Because I'm a hawk.'"

Tikka jumped up from beside me, her eyes wide open. "What happened then? What happened?"

Nahani closed her eyes. "Go to sleep, little bears. Go to sleep."

CHAPTER TWO

The Big Bad River

We bounded down from the mountains, and soon the hard shale under our pads began to soften as we loped along in the stunted mountain pines. The moist air was full of new smells and, as the timber thickened, a symphony of warning calls from the birds to beasts alerted all those who lived in the valley that a grizzly was in the area.

Nahani's ears patrolled the winds for any intruders as a musky smell drifted through the spruce trees. Mother stood on her hind legs, drawing the scent in. As we stepped cautiously around the roots of one large hemlock tree, Tikka was the first to notice the claw marks that ripped into the southern face of the great tree. A big grizzly had reached high into the branches and clawed his warning that this forest belonged to him.

Tikka walked up beside me. "This place sure is creepy," I whispered.

"Yes, it's got a different feel. That's for sure," Tikka gulped and added, "Maybe we'll meet One-Eye."

Mother turned. "Quiet!" she hissed.

I snuck closer to Tikka. "If I see One-Eye, I think I'll eat him." Tikka could only roll her eyes at me and push out her bottom lip. I shot back with my best crazy face and chomped my teeth.

Over several days and nights of travel, the big river's clatter grew from the buzz of a bee to a constant rushing, like the hard rains of spring. Long warm days turned the trickling alpine streams into bristling creeks, and Mother's hunger drove us on. Once we arrived at river's edge, Nahani was careful, but her hunger was so strong that she was almost in a salmon trance. Tikka and I waited in the bog willows along the riverbank. Mother's eyes scanned the gravel bars for danger. "Not a sound, you two. No matter what."

We dropped down, huddled next to each other. We listened carefully, and as the winds changed, we could smell other grizzlies feeding in the area. We squeezed in tight and said nothing. We waited. A salmon fell through the grass, still flopping. Mother pounced, and her sharp teeth peeled the skin away from the fish as the salmon's eggs dripped into the grass. In a craze, she chomped into the salmon's head, sucking out the delicious brains. She devoured it completely, leaving nothing for us. She stood up, listening closely. Nahani scanned all around and quietly disappeared back towards the river.

By the time we watched her gulp her third fish, Tikka and I were fighting over any scraps left. They smelled so good! Soon the grass parted before us again and there was Nahani, this time with two wriggling salmon in her mouth. She dropped them and said, "Try it."

That was the first day we dined on lovely salmon. Their oily taste was like no other. My favorite parts were the eggs and brains. Oh, so good! We played this hide-and-wait-for-salmon game for weeks, and Nahani started to get quite plump. Tikka and I were rounding out too, and our coats became shiny and full. We had seen lots of other female bears, some with cubs and some without, and the river kept giving her bounty as the days grew shorter.

We always slept above the river in the thick birch forest. The ground was soft and dry. It felt safe, and the breeze was just strong enough that we could smell anything approaching. It was our safe little home under the silvery canopy of the trees. As the twilight faded, I could never have imagined that this would become my darkest night—a night that would give birth to an ever-present shadow that would follow me as far as my journey would take me.

Our peace was disrupted by a low, menacing growl. I sprang to Nahani's side. I knew that this was something to really fear. Mother stepped cautiously towards the sound. She extended her snout into the dark and roared like a thundercloud. Her shoulders flared and her teeth flashed white in the blackness. Just then, for only a second, I saw him—a huge grizzly, much older than any bear I had ever seen before. His hard-eyed face was cut up, and his lower lip hung from his jaw, a relic of a recent battle. Without warning, he charged. Nahani met him with everything she had, and the violent roars shook me to the core. The massive male bit down on Nahani's neck, pulling away a chunk of her hair with his barbaric bite. Nahani slashed her claws over the intruder's eyes, and he bellowed in pain. The cub killer turned toward me and Tikka, and Mother sunk her fangs into his muscled shoulder as thick streams of blood poured over his chest.

"Run!" Mother yelled between the savage screams.

Tikka scrambled like a chipmunk straight up the hill, and in an instant, I could no longer hear or see her anymore. I was lost and alone in the dark, climbing over stumps and rocks looking for Tikka. I could still hear the fighting in the distance. Something big was crashing through the timber below me. I squeezed under the broken branches of the wind-fallen trees and followed a small rabbit trail into a creek bed just off the main river. My heart pounded and sheer panic gripped my entire body. I fled into the nearby underbrush and decided to do what Nahani had told us to do. I was going to be quiet and not move a muscle.

For the remainder of that night, my eyes and ears strained against the darkness and the usual sounds of the forest as I searched for any sign of my family. When the sun finally appeared, fear had settled in as my new lifelong companion.

Something big splashed in the creek behind me. My fear made me shrink; becoming as small as possible, I pressed myself into the cool, damp moss. There I wept, wondering if I would ever see my mother and sister again.

Why had we come to this terrible place? I decided that I hated other grizzlies, and I promised myself that if I made it through this, I would stay away from other grizzly bears and not travel along any salmon rivers anymore. My mountain blueberries were safe, and they were good enough for me.

A stick snapped in the distance. There was something big approaching from behind me. Trembling, I covered my face with my paws, wanting to hide from whatever it was. With eyes clenched tight, I hoped that it would not notice me and would simply walk on by.

Then, something cold and wet reached through the bushes and sniffed along my back. It touched along my shoulders, and I braced for the beast's brutal bite.

"Are you okay?" I looked up. It was Mother.

She looked terrible. Her eyes were almost swollen shut. Her head hung low. Gaping claw wounds around her neck showed dried rings of blood from her battle. Weakly she whispered, "We must leave the river now."

We walked for the rest of the afternoon and continued into the night. Hours later, just before dawn, Mother turned and softly told me what I already knew.

"Tikka is gone."

CHAPTER THREE

The Wolves of Winter

For the next few days, we trudged back up into the mountains. I moved as if through a fog, and I felt a kind of dull poison welling up inside me. This dullness sapped my spirit as my mind replayed that horrible night over and over again. Our pace was steady, but Nahani laboured behind me. She was looking weaker every day.

"We need more food before hibernation. I don't want to die an ice bear," she said, and then continued.

When I was a cub, I heard stories of an ice bear—or, as the old ones call them, jingle bears: a jolly name for a terrible thing. When a grizzly's long hair drags through the deep snow, crystals of ice clump together at the ends. They say if you ever hear a jingle on the wind, you'd better run and hide, lest you face the madness of the ice bear. The story goes that long ago, a grizzly unprepared for winter was hunting late in the season, desperate for food, when he managed to kill a yearling caribou. He had run it into a swamp and made a clean, quick kill, grasping a second chance at life. He stuffed his prize beneath an upturned tree, for he knew the wolf packs were patrolling the valley. He walked a large circle around his kill, smelling and watching for any who might steal his last meal. He picked up the pace as he headed back, but when he returned, only the scent of blood remained. He turned, growling into the silence. He put his nose to the ground and followed the iron scent, which led him to the base of a Tamarack tree. He peered up into the branches.

Anger boiled through his body at the sight of the sleek, dark-colored cougar whose paw was placed territorially on the hide of the caribou that was slumped over the branches. The grizzly bellowed, and the cougar sat still, high in the tree, hissing down his contempt.

The grizzly tore furiously at the branches, but in his weakened state, his body was simply too big to maneuver up the tree. Some say that the bear sat there for three days and nights, watching his prize slowly vanish into the cat's eager mouth, transfixed by his focused hatred while the snows drifted in around him. Chilling white powder became his den until, skinny, mad, and burning with hunger, he broke free.

He roamed on, foggy-eyed, longing for any morsel of meat. He came upon a human and twelve sled dogs, and he charged at them, downing one dog. Just as the warm blood reached the jingle bear's tongue, the human's smoke pole exploded outward, thundering through the forest, causing a cloud of black ravens to burst from the treetops. The jingle bear reared and fell to the ground.

I thought often of this fable as the snow now fell day and night, and our stomachs began to shrink. We traveled higher into the mountains, taking turns breaking trail. Somehow our luck had to change. I needed only to look at Nahani's gaunt frame to realize we weren't nearly ready for hibernation.

The clucking of ptarmigan travels well on the wind, but most grizzlies don't bother hunting them. Nahani, however, had an ingenious method. It was a case of herding and ambushing, and with patience and focus, we managed a few good feeds. Combined with a few rabbits and gophers, we finally had the fat layers necessary for hibernation.

Nahani dug our den. Like always, she chose a cool spot near a small thicket where the ground was not too rocky. Nahani's strong shoulders moved earth and shaped a den with amazing speed. Two days later and the den was ready. I crawled in after her to take a look.

Just then, my nose caught something I had never smelled before. I was about to stand for a better sniff when Mother backed herself out of the den. She stood tall, searching. Her posture and breathing changed. She was ready for trouble.

That's when I saw my first wolf. I knew from the many stories Mother told us that we were bitter enemies. There were seven of them: some black, some grey, and one almost pure white. But the largest wolf, the one leading the pack, was midnight black except for a blaze of white that ran from one eye over half his muzzle.

As they approached, the wolves skulked like shadowy monsters. Mother hissed, "Get to the back of the den. They're here for you."

I scrambled through the tunnel to the back wall of dirt and snow. I waited. I could hear Mother's growls and the padding of dozens of paws as the wolves circled the den, moving and testing. Growls long and deep came from her throat as her backside protected the den entrance. The wolves were on the hunt, ruthless kings of winter.

After what seemed a long time, I heard a wolf's howl and then the thud of paws running on snow.

Nahani turned and slipped back into the den. She lay with her nose close to the entrance.

"They're gone."

"Why did they come here? Why did they want us?"

"I think they saw your smaller tracks and thought they could separate us."

"Who was that black wolf, Mother?"

"His name is Eleven-Thirty. They call him that because he's not quite midnight black—he's more like Eleven-Thirty. He is the Alpha male of the Snake River wolf pack. Few creatures have the pace and stamina of wolves, but someday, when you're old enough, I can promise you that even Eleven-Thirty won't be any concern to a grand grizzly like you, Rumble Bear."

Mother placed a few more branches and scraped the snow together to totally plug the entrance. Eleven-Thirty's chilling howl rolled over the mountains. Winter was here, and the wolves now ruled. The world was small again, and my mind raced.

I missed Tikka. I tried to be quiet and to be strong, but I felt very alone.

Nahani curled up beside me. "I miss her too," she said knowingly.

CHAPTER FOUR

Ripping Out Your Roots

The spring of my second year started much like the first. After breaking free from the pocket of warmth we had called home all winter, hungry, we trotted down from the mountains into spring's green grasses. Soon we felt our strength return, and we both looked forward to the endless bounties of a new season.

This year felt different. I was older and stronger, ready to travel greater distances. I relished the excitement of new smells, sights, and creatures. Nahani was a patient and wise teacher. Her tales of the natural world always reminded me to listen and feel the world around me.

The topic of Tikka never arose, but I do remember one special moment. Nahani was stretching her neck and shoulders, sniffing the wind for what might lurk in the thick timber in front of us.

Without any thought, I blurted, "Why are male grizzlies so dangerous? Why are they so unpredictable?"

Mother turned and looked me square in the eyes. "Legacy."

"What do you mean?"

Her voice was clear and calm. "Rumble, our species and our history are forged by the great grizzlies of the past. Only the strongest, most courageous, and cunning grizzlies will mate, and it is only that great bear's bloodlines that will endure."

My thoughts drifted, imagining what my own father might be like. Was he strong? Was he brave? I thought this topic might madden Mother, for she never spoke of him.

I hesitated. "What was my father like?"

Quiet. All was quiet. I watched Nahani's eyes as she thought.

I lowered myself down onto my belly, placed my chin between my paws and waited.

Mother's voice echoed off the big cottonwood trees. I remember her eyes, locked on to some distant point in the sky.

"When your father was in his prime, he was the most powerful grizzly on the marsh flats. His reputation carried far and wide, and his bloodlines branched out into every part of the world. He was the lord of the entire valley, and few bears would think of even approaching him."

"Wow!" This was so exciting. I needed to hear about every adventure, every brave battle my father fought and every mystic place he roamed.

"Where is he now?" I asked.

Mother pressed her claws into the moss. "I heard he was in a great battle somewhere in the mountains. I heard too that a powerful grizzly named Growler killed your father." She added, "I understand that now Growler walks as the lord of the marsh flats."

I nuzzled in closer to Mother. "Am I much like my father?" I asked.

Nahani's face softened as she gazed into the distance. "In some ways," she replied.

I closed my eyes. I knew that death was the one element that always seemed to shut down my booming imagination, bringing me back to what was real. Yes, these great tales of Mother Nature inspired many bears to become real grizzlies. But I had learned very young that these exciting stories always forgot to mention all the fear, pain, and worry that followed like fleas on your back.

No. I figured the best way was the easy way. "I will never go to these flats that you speak of, Mother. My life is just fine here with you. I don't need any other grizzlies in my world."

She turned and looked me in the eyes. "Rumble, everything in life changes. That's the one thing you can always count on."

Summer was one long feast. We kept to ourselves, hunting and travelling great distances. We spent a few weeks cruising the woodland like ghosts. We even managed to take down an old bison who put up a spirited fight but was no match for what Nahani called the famous-grizzly-windpipe-bite.

I knew salmon season would start soon and that before long, Nahani's salmon hunger would again awaken. She walked with a bounce in her step. "It's time we went back to the river for the great salmon feast, Rumble boy."

"I don't want to go, Mother. Why don't we stick with the squirrels and gophers? Maybe we'll get lucky with another bison. Throw in a few weeks of blueberries and before you know it, we're home, fat and happy, for a nice safe hibernation!"

Nahani was hot-mad. Her hair stood on end along her back. "You have to take your place along the riverbank if you want to survive another year. Rumble, you're a grizzly bear. Start acting like one."

My face warmed with shame. I knew in my heart she was wrong about this.

As she began to wade into the Snake River towards the salmon bonanza, I paused and tried to find the courage not to follow, but it took only one lonely look around for me to reluctantly give in.

After days of walking, the sound of that rumbling river greeted our approach. Nahani picked up the pace. The great river reeked of salmon fermenting along the gravel bars. Bears of all sizes fed ravenously on fish.

This bad place made my nerves quiver, but my appetite for salmon was getting stronger. I noticed that Nahani was also changing. She spoke less, and wandered off on her own sometimes without looking to see if I was still with her.

We found a place along the river where the water flowed at just the right depth over the rocks. We chased and herded the fish just like ptarmigan into the rocky shore.

Over the next few weeks, the salmon came in waves. When the fishing was good, life followed suit. One evening, Nahani told me about the marsh flats further down the valley.

"One day, when you are ready, you will have to make your journey down to the grizzlies' flats. You'll have to be cautious, for one of my old sow friends told me that a new bear named Tobaldi is now king of the flats. Rumble Bear, you must realize that the strongest grizzlies will always take from the weaker, so be ready to play your part, whatever that may be. You must believe that you are a great grizzly and that thousands of years of grand grizzly blood flows through your veins. Of all my cubs, you are the one bear always dreaming, always gazing somewhere off into the distance. I know your mind is bursting with questions that I fear I simply cannot answer. My advice, Rumble Bear, is that whatever you're searching for, it isn't waiting for you somewhere out in the world. The answers are all inside you."

With fourteen sockeye salmon in the belly today, I fell asleep thinking about what Nahani had told me.

When I awoke at first light, Mother was gone. I was frantic. I looked up and down the river. I checked the side-hills, sniffed all the game trails, but she was gone. The fog rolled in with that old feeling of loneliness, and it seemed to nest right in my bones. I searched day and night for over a week. The salmon-run over, I decided to travel back into the mountains, back to our old den. I just knew she would be there, and I was sure there was a good reason why she had vanished from the river.

I travelled mainly at night now. I found the dark made me feel too lonely to sleep, and I couldn't tear my mind from Mother's absence. I followed our old well-worn trails. One afternoon, I stopped by the base of the steep grey cliffs where Nahani, Tikka, and I had rested all those months ago. A layer of soft moss had grown over the old bed Mother had carefully sculpted from dirt, a safe piece of the world for our little family. Tears matted the fur on my face as I gazed at the contours in the mossy bed where I'd swear I could make out the outlines of where each of us had rested together long ago.

I pushed my nose to the moss to see if I could still smell those wonderful moments, but there was nothing. I fell into the bed and closed my eyes. Painful thoughts cascaded through me and threatened to push me deeper and deeper into the ground. It was the all-knowing lady herself, Mother Nature, who felt my pain and brought me back with a faint call that bounced along the barren cliffs.

As I looked skyward into nothingness, I recognized the distinct hunting call of the elusive peregrine falcon. I watched the solitary white bird patrol her cliffs and listened as she called out to her prey, daring any roosting birds to try to out-fly the fastest bird in the world.

She was the daredevil of the skies. Mother had told us about the great falcon's courage and how her kind often hunted birds twice their size, knocking them out of the sky with curled talons as she rolled and dove into her prey. I listened now and could hear her voice bring panic to the residents of the cliffs. She was a patient hunter, toying with her prey, urging something hidden in the crannies to take desperate flight.

Finally, one foolish jay sprang out low along the cliff wall, his wings beating full speed. The white falcon turned with purpose and hovered high above. Gazing down, she lined up her victim, tucked her wings, and dropped out of the sky like a rock.

I stood to watch this marvel of nature. The jay was almost down into the safety of the trees. He only had a few hundred more feet to go. But the white bullet was plummeting at full speed, wings quivering. Bang! A brilliant burst of blue feathers floated down and I watched the great falcon depart with her prize still twitching in her talons.

When I finally arrived at our old den, I waited. Days passed. Then weeks. I hunted the alpine for any sign of Mother, but nothing. She was gone, and as the snows deepened all around my den, I looked down the long slope one last time and then crawled into the dark. I eventually fell asleep, wondering if I would ever see her again.

CHAPTER FIVE

At Some Point in Life, Your Monster Will Appear

Spring of my third year. When I awoke, I looked around the den for Mother, but she was not there. I wondered whether she was okay. I felt the fog well up again in my brain, and I tried to will it away, to rouse myself. I wanted change, but somehow knew I would be the only one who could bring it about.

The thing was, I simply didn't know how.

When I emerged, I was hungry. A newfound lust for meat consumed my stomach. I wandered down the valley and gorged on vegetation and a few squirrels, but my hunger remained. I could feel that my body had changed. My neck was longer, and my shoulders were much broader than last season.

As I crossed a small pond, I heard a sharp thud on the water. I looked over, and saw this most peculiar animal. It had a small head like a gopher, a bear's hair, and a huge tail like a flat mushroom cap. The animal slapped the water again—whap! His scent was that of a hundred rotten pine squirrels all bubbling in the sun. I climbed out of the pond and followed my nose.

I moved slowly and saw a huge pile of sticks in one corner of the pond. "Must be his home," I thought. I decided to watch him quietly for the rest of the day.

Next morning, I saw the creature emerge with a large branch clenched in his huge teeth, swimming down to the far end of the pond. "What on earth is he doing?" I muttered as I watched, watching him return over and over to the same part of the pond to carefully place more sticks and limbs. The intrigue of this creature made me forget my hunger momentarily, but after several moments of spectating, the creature's movements became predictable, I lost interest, and my hunger was once again painfully apparent. I needed meat, and I would do anything to get it.

That evening, in total darkness, I walked down to the long line of mud and trees so carefully placed along the far end of the pond, and I tore into it. I ripped with all my might and eventually pulled the debris away, dragging some of the trees up onto the bank. In the darkness, I could feel the water begin to rush past my legs.

I felt my way up the bank and bedded down behind a large pile of boulders with the still-wet pile of branches I'd pulled from the pond. As I fell asleep, I remembered Mother telling me about this strange animal she had called a beaver.

That morning, I awoke to a splashing sound. I peered out past the boulders, and there was my beaver, briskly repairing his dam. I waited patiently, and finally he crawled out of the water. He was much bigger than I had imagined. The wind was perfect. I remember Mother always saying to me, "Hunt with the wind in your face."

He slipped back into the water with one of the branches and carefully mended the hole I had made. When he came to retrieve the next branch, I was going to take him.

When he pulled himself onto the bank, I felt my heart pounding. This was the largest animal I had ever hunted alone. This was the real food I needed to survive. There he was—ten steps away now. Eight steps. I charged. He started desperately back towards the pond as I sunk my teeth into his head. He tried to pull himself away, but the taste of blood spurred me on. The kill was quick. I dragged him into the thick bush.

I feasted like a king. I ate all day, and that night I buried what was left so no other bear would smell my prize. I felt good. A new energy seemed to be flowing into my body. Real meat—not just fish—seemed then something essential. I smiled. This was what it felt like to be a real grizzly. I was proud, and wished Mother could have seen me become a great and cunning hunter. I wondered where she was and whether she was okay.

At that moment, I realized Mother was probably at the marsh flats. Maybe that was what she meant when she told me that one day, when I was ready, I must go there.

It was still spring and the creeks were running fast. My long journey was not going to be easy, as I didn't even know exactly where the marsh flats were. But as I set off, I knew instinctively that I was heading in the right direction. My soul seemed to guide me.

I knew for sure that my instincts hadn't misled me when I encountered my first mature male grizzly along a deep rutted game trail. I generally stayed off of the trails because Mother had told me that they were used by larger grizzlies. He had a slow, deliberate gait and walked with a distinctive head bob from side to side. His claws were massive, and his shoulders and chest were the largest I had ever seen. When the wind changed direction, he stopped, lifted his head quizzically, and sniffed the air. He knew I was nearby. He stood on his hind legs and peered in my direction.

I was transfixed. His eyes had no fear. I quietly turned and started to run. After a few moments, I glanced back and realized he was not following me. I stopped on a gravel bank and pondered my next move.

Walking back toward the game trails, I caught a faint whiff of a familiar smell.

It couldn't be; could it? I pulled in as much air as I could. Yes! It was true—the distinct scent of Mother! She was close.

I hurried my pace as I headed toward the marsh. I wanted to tell her about my hunt and show her that I was becoming a real grizzly and would leave a legacy after all.

As I entered the marsh, I saw grizzlies in the distance. I was sure Mother would be there, but as I approached, I could sense fear in the wind. These were not friendly bears. They were gigantic, powerful males. I could see about ten bears of different ages and sizes, but there were no females around. They seemed agitated as they stood apart watching and studying each other's moves and sounds.

None of the bears took much notice as I approached. I started to walk more slowly. I wanted to show my size and indicate that I was not afraid. What I wanted most was to ask if any of them had seen my Mother.

I decided to walk towards one of the smaller grizzlies standing at the edge of the group. As I came closer, the bears watched me carefully, and one smaller bear moved away. One who seemed to be about my age turned and looked at me. He growled and popped his jaws.

"Hey! I'm not looking for a fight. I'm looking for a female bear."

He sneered. "That's what we're all doing here—looking for females. What's wrong with you? Are you stupid?"

"No, I'm looking for my Mother. I think she is here somewhere."

"Well," he said, "all the females are over in that area, but I wouldn't go over there."

"Why not?"

"Because Tobaldi is over there and only he spends time with the females."

"Yes, but I just want to quickly see my Mother and let her know I'm alright."

He looked at me with a sly grin. "Well then, you should head over. I'm sure it will be just fine."

I set off almost running. I knew Mother would be so happy to see me. She would be proud that I had become a true grizzly. I was so overwhelmed with thoughts and feelings that I was not aware that I was entering a new, strange, and very dangerous place.

I approached the trail entrance. The dark, thick canopy cast cold shadows on the ground, but after a few twists and turns, the path opened up and became suddenly awash with sunshine. This was a paradise. The fragrant, lush, dewy grasses and crystal stream moistened the air, and the sun poured its beautiful rays across the open field. Only a hundred meters away I saw two female bears clawing at a fallen log. They looked so peaceful and relaxed. Again I smelled the air for any hint of Mother. Nothing.

I casually approached the two bears. One had lustrous, cinnamon-coloured fur and was around four or five years old. The other was the same age, blonde around the head and shoulders but with dark brown fur blending out along her back.

"Hello! My name is Rumble Bear." I pawed casually at the dirt. "I'm friendly and mean you no harm."

They said nothing, and continued to lick at the odd bug that popped out of the rotten wood. I moved a little closer. "Could you help me? I'm looking for my Mother. Her name is Nahani."

The cinnamon bear spat and turned her head towards me. "Get out of here. Are you crazy? If Tobaldi sees you here, he'll kill you on the spot."

It's funny, looking back, to think that until that day I had not even considered Tobaldi a threat. I remember that I was sure he would understand that I was no trouble.

The cinnamon bear quickly scanned the willows, and again turned on me. "Get out of here, you fool." She sauntered away.

I looked into the eyes of the blonde bear. Her calm, kind demeanor was markedly different from the few other female bears I had met.

"What is your name?" I asked her.

"Baja." She half-turned to me. "You are very different from other bears I've met. You seem unafraid. Most bears who arrive here are consumed with fear because of Tobaldi. Just his name scares almost every male grizzly I know, turning them into trembling cowards running to live alone in the cold shadows of the forest."

I felt great. I always knew I was a special bear. It was nice that she recognized my potential. This was attention I could get used to. Mother fell from my mind.

Baja and I talked and play-fought for what felt like all afternoon. She loved it when I pretended I couldn't see her, and she would roll into a ball laughing whenever I fell over her as if I was an old blind bear. Meeting Baja was a wonderful gift. After just those few playful hours, I thought that I wanted to spend every day with her. I wanted to show her so many things, to tell her all my stories, to travel together and share fantastic adventures. I was soon to learn, however, that a great bear's journey is made up of much more than lazy summer days with a new friend.

When my nose first inhaled that scent, I could never have imagined how close my journey would come to ending that day.

I wouldn't have believed a grizzly that large could move with the speed of a lynx. It happened so fast. I tried to turn and run, but before I could move, Tobaldi's fangs dug deep into my neck. The pain was like fire and brambles and a thousand mud wasps all at once.

Tobaldi was so strong that when he mashed his paw onto the side of my head, I was thrown backwards. When I rolled, all I could see was a hulking mass of teeth, fur, and muscle, punctured by two cruel eyes. I started zig-zagging through the small stand of trees. The sound of his roar drove my claws through the dirt as I desperately willed myself away.

I felt blood coursing in thick lines down my face, and when I exhaled, blood shot out from my muzzle, splattering back on me as I ran. I thought I was pulling away, but I soon realized that while I was running around the trees, Tobaldi was simply plowing them down.

Just as I cornered one of the larger trees in the area, Tobaldi clawed at my back leg and I was hurled into the air. I landed and rolled in a burst of tree bark, coming to my feet for a second before Tobaldi smashed me to the ground. With a roar, he bit down hard on my left ear. I remember hearing his low growl and looking up into his blood-red eyes.

The more I pulled back against the tree away from him, the louder he groaned. He clenched his jaw, tearing at me. I screamed. I was going to die, and I was going to leave no mark on the world—no legacy. Tobaldi seemed to sense my hopelessness, and his bite loosened.

"I must fight!" I thought. "I must try!" Tobaldi jerked his massive head away from me, leaving only one of his dagger-sharp claws holding my back leg. I could hear his breathing slowing and realized this was my one and only chance. I had to try!

I jumped to my feet, braced my back legs, and drove my front claws blindly onto Tobaldi's face. He roared in pain as I tore away, crashing wildly through the brush. I glanced back to see Tobaldi howling in pain. I was running for my life.

CHAPTER SIX

SEARCHING FOR MY NEW ISLAND

Why Tobaldi never chased me any farther that day, I don't know. Looking back, I think I just didn't really matter that much to him.

With time, my physical scars eventually healed. My tattered ear hung down like an old moose ear, and strips along my neck where the hair grew in lighter shades served as grim reminders of that terrible day. I vowed I would never return to the marsh flats again.

Something had changed in me. I awoke every morning filled with dread, and I felt as if something or some part of me was missing. I wandered out of the valleys and the mountains that I knew. I hated those places now. I wanted to find a place where I could recapture the sense of peace I had felt before fighting Tobaldi.

Even food did not bring me joy. That terrible day played over and over in my mind. What could I have done differently? Why had I been so naive?

The only part of that day I wanted to remember was the time I had spent with Baja. I would often think of her, and at night I would dream that maybe, someday, we would meet again.

I fed for a while on the cloudberries that grew alongside a small creek, and slept beneath a stand of pines, hoping to forget my sorrows.

"There must be a place for me somewhere," I blurted out loud.

"Wow! You must be the most miserable grizzly bear I've ever seen."

I stood and glanced into the trees above, and there sat an old blue grouse basking in the sun.

I looked closer. "No way! It can't be. Are you One-Eye?"

"That's what they call me. I'm always amazed just how far that story of me and that red hawk has travelled. Usually I just watch grizzlies. I don't often speak to one, but I must say, you look like one beaten-down bear. You look like you're carrying a lot on those big shoulders of yours. If I were you, I would shake that off pretty quick before it becomes permanent."

"I wish I could. I'm searching for answers."

"Oh, a searching soul, are you?"

I shrugged, unsure.

"Well, what is the most important question you need answered?"

"I guess I need to know where I belong. I'm looking for a safe place where I feel comfortable and don't have to worry so much."

"Sounds like a nice place. You'll have to tell me if you find it."

"I'm beginning to believe it simply doesn't exist."

"You remind me of a cougar I met many years ago. He too was a searching soul. He was born on an island down on the coast, and as he grew he would walk around his large island, staring out to sea for something new, something different. His island was wonderful. Lots of food and space, and the other cougars he knew loved it and would never want or need to leave. But this cougar was different. His gaze was always out to sea—looking, searching for that something that was missing, and with every new moon his searching soul grew more restless. Until one day, the ocean was so still and flat and calm that he was unable to resist any longer.

He had heard legends that hundreds of incredible islands lay to the west. Islands with bounties and places and things so incredible that they would fill your soul with pure joy."

I knew just how that cougar felt. "So what did he do?"

"When he entered the ocean, his only thoughts were to swim west, for since he was a cub he had heard legends about islands to the west. He swam the rest of that day, and, as darkness fell, he paused to look back at his island. He found it was no longer visible. Vague feelings of regret crept into his mind. These glorious islands were farther than he'd thought, but he willed himself on through the darkness. Morning brought great thirst. Fear, worry, and regret swam alongside him well into his second day. The ocean was deep and cold."

"'What if? What if? What if?' thumped through his head. He thought of his home, of the delicious deer and cool, clear streams. Here, suspended among the waves, he found himself wishing for his old island.

"The empty blue horizon was all he could see. He knew then that he was just a foolish cougar caught in the middle of the ocean. 'What have I done to myself?' he thought. Three more days passed, the saltwater drawing all the moisture from his eyes and mouth. He was, by now, floating rather than swimming. He realized that only the current would shape his fate.

"Knowing only scant hours lay between him and the other side, he said aloud, 'Please, give me an island.'

"A speck in the distance caught his eye. He shook his head to clear the salt from his eyes and scanned the horizon. There it was! A small dot in the distance. The cougar paddled desperately. Faint hope gave him strength. Head high, he forged on and the speck grew bigger.

"'Please, let it be an island.'

"The current was in his favor, and gradually he drew closer. Hour after weary hour passed. The distance seemed to stretch out ahead of him.

Twice he rolled onto his side and swam in pitiful circles until the sharp sting of desperate fear spurred him on.

"When he washed up on the beach, his body had nothing left. He dragged himself onto the sand and immediately collapsed into a deep sleep.

"When he awoke, bone-weary, he foraged a few small crabs and bird eggs and found water. He finally had the strength to explore his new island. His joy quickly vanished when, within a few short hours, he found himself at the very spot where he had washed ashore. After a deep breath, he looked out to sea and thought he heard the ocean whisper, 'Come on, cougar. Come swim with me.'

"Enjoy your search, grizzly bear." With that, old One-Eye launched into flight. He soared like a hawk. His soul seemed to have found the answers it had sought, and he moved with purpose and surety. He swept into the bluest part of the sky and disappeared.

As I wandered along the shoreline of a frigid deep lake that evening, I wondered if I too was a searching soul. That cougar's journey somehow seemed familiar to me, but I hoped my life would not turn out like that poor cat's. As the night grew darker, I began to curse old One-Eye.

He had never really finished his story. Was the cougar still swimming around the ocean, or did he stay and make do with that lonely little island? As I ventured into the night, I knew just how that cougar had felt.

With each new day, my travels uncovered new strange things. One afternoon, I heard something far in the distance. The tone, rhythmic and unsettling, grew louder and then suddenly stopped.

I found a distinct trail cored through the wilderness. A flat grey space cut through the warm greens and browns of the bush. I hoped I would never meet whatever animal made this game trail. Still, my curiosity led me onward.

I approached, muscles taut. Not a sound now. I looked around. Nothing. All was still. The cut looked like something had smashed through the rocks and placed them in a neat, straight line. Whatever animal this was, he liked his trails to be direct. There was no thought for Mother Nature's contours.

I sniffed at the black rock on the trail and pushed it, but it didn't move an inch. It had a strange taste, like salt and oil. Though I'd never tasted this before, it was something I instantly craved.

Morning came and my nose caught the sweet smell of something rotting in the distance. I knew this grey game trail was something to stay away from, but that wonderful smell must be only a few miles away. It was simply too much to resist.

Mother once told me about these dangerous invaders that would on occasion journey into the land of the grizzlies. She warned that they were loud, smelly, and, though weak, were immensely cunning. She said that humans and bears were creatures that God never intended should meet. We were simply too different.

I remember her simple rule: a grizzly should always be humble and stay away from humans.

The smell of putrid rot was now smashing me in the face. It must be a huge animal lying dead with its guts and fat fizzing away, tenderizing in the sun, waiting just for me.

I was travelling fast, my nose pulling me through the bush, when the forest opened like a curtain and I saw a place of forgotten and unwanted treasures. I had found the local dump. Food was piled up like it had been dropped from the sky. I walked into it ready to feast, but I recognized nothing. I searched through rainbows of colours: yellow, green, white. But they had no taste. Finally, I found something. It was sweet and thick. I reached my tongue as far as I could into a vessel, getting every drop.

"Hey, bear! That will give you the bellyache like you could never imagine!"

I spun around to see a medium-sized, sickly-looking grizzly only a few stumps away. I let out a long, low growl.

He looked at me with pure fear and started to back away. "Look, I'm not here to fight. I'm just here for my lunch. I usually wait for a few trucks to come by. There's lots here for everyone."

This bear was different from others of my kind. His eyes were duller, and he seemed incomplete in some way.

"Who are you?" I called to him.

"I'm Boulder. I live here at the dump. You know, that's motor oil you're drinking. I once drank three bottles of that stuff, but wow, it was like bad mushrooms sitting in my stomach. When it arrived at the other end, it wrought pure vengeance." He walked closer, lifting an eyebrow. "Who are you?"

"I'm Rumble Bear."

"I see you're new in the area. My buddy and I are the only grizzlies around here. Most bears steer clear of this place. There are a lot of black bears in the area, but when we see them, we chase them off."

I turned as I heard a faint sound in the distance.

Boulder suddenly turned too. "Hey, truck's coming! We've got to move right now."

Boulder scuttled away quickly, and I followed. "Hurry! We don't want to be spotted," Boulder urged.

Back in the bush, we stopped. "Why do we run from these trucks? Are they furious?"

Boulder looked me up and down slowly. "I see you're a wild bear. I'm a bit more advanced than you," he sniffed, "in that I live next to humans. You see, they bring their refuse here and as long as I stay away from them, they seem to leave me alone. I've only really had one major event here in three seasons."

"An event?" I asked.

"Well, once a human came to the dump, and I started to move away but he spotted me. He was travelling with these wolf-like creatures he called 'dogs.' Well, these dogs are pretty loyal to the humans, but they really aren't the thing to worry about—they're small and scare easy. It's the smoke poles you've got to look out for."

"What's a smoke pole?"

"It's a long tube that the humans often carry, and when it is released, it's like the greatest thunderstorm you've ever heard. But that's not where the danger lies. It's what flies through the air that's bad.

"Imagine something only the size of a bee but that travels faster than any other creature in the world."

I laughed out loud. "Even faster than the great falcon in a full dive?"

Boulder nodded slowly. "It's so fast that all you hear is it zing past you, but this tiny little thing will hit you so hard that it can knock you out cold or even kill you."

There was a silence. Boulder seemed to shake himself off. "Come on, let's go meet Chopper."

Chopper was big and strong, and had seen a few more seasons than Boulder and me. He was dark, and his face showed several deep scars, tokens of past battles. I got to know Chopper as the summer wore on, and by the time fall rolled around, I was happy to call him leader.

As fall's cool night painted the trees around us red, I realized that yes, I was surviving here, and yes, it was nice to be around other bears again. But I'd noticed that this routine of sleeping in the bush during the day and gorging at the dump at dusk was affecting my mind and body somehow. I would occasionally eat something that might make me sick for a few days, but this life was much easier than living like the wild grizzlies. It was safer too—Tobaldi haunted only my dreams, and from there he could never hurt me again.

When the first snows began to fall, the three of us could feel the sleepiness begin to take hold. Eventually, we all said our goodbyes and decided to meet back at the dump in the spring.

I travelled east for about a day until I found a large aspen blown over. The roots had pulled away and uncovered a small cave.

I decided this would do. This was my winter den.

CHAPTER SEVEN

BATTLE BY THE OUTHOUSE

My hibernation was terrible. I never fell into that deep sleep that grizzlies cherish over the winter. I awoke many times, and the cold seemed to sink into my flesh more than ever before.

I should have stayed in the den longer, but my hunger chased me out into the heavy snowpack of early spring. As I trudged to the dump, I noticed that my body had not grown as it did in years past and that my muscles were not as I knew they should be. When I arrived, most of the dump was still covered in brown, flecked snow.

I could see lots of tracks, mostly of rabbits and mice, and I noticed a few broken grouse feathers lying in the snow where a bobcat had managed to find a late winter meal. I could see a fresh pile of garbage, so I made my way over for my first bite of food in months. I found some scraps of fish in cans and eventually uncovered a good-sized piece of rotting meat. I felt my energy regenerate over the following days, and eventually Boulder and Chopper appeared. Although Boulder was thin, he seemed to be in good spirits and was looking forward to the warm, sunny days of summer.

Chopper, on the other hand, complained about everything: his den wasn't right and the cold winter made all his aches and pains worse. He often spoke of his days back when he lived in the wild and dined on salmon and moose calves. He claimed that he too had been to the marsh flats, and that, back in his prime, he'd been king of the whole area. I knew that none of that was true, but since Boulder had never been to the marsh flats and seemed to love these tall tales, I decided to keep quiet. These boasts weren't hurting anyone.

Our little bear gang enjoyed spring together, and the three of us became close friends. I told them about my run-in with Tobaldi, about my cunning beaver kill, and I even spoke of my sister and of what had happened at the great salmon river.

Life was simple and uneventful. But as summer approached, things started to change.

I was sleeping when I heard the boom. I jumped up, tensing as another boom followed and then an even louder one. Boulder raced away in a flat-out dash, crashing through the bush, and I could hear humans and dogs chasing him.

The three of us scattered, but a few hours later we all met up at our favorite sandy patch by a small stream a few miles from the dump.

Chopper was hunched over a log, visibly shaken, as Boulder paced, smelling and listening. I approached them. "What happened?"

Chopper turned on me, his eyes narrowed. "What do you think happened?"

Boulder was shivering. "The s-s-smoke pole," he said, "It almost g-g-got me."

"The smoke pole darn near killed him," said Chopper. "This is bad. We are in trouble if the humans get angry. They're going to come back, and they won't leave until there's a dead grizzly at their feet."

"Come on, let's calm down," I urged. "We just need to give it some time. If we wait a few days, everything will calm down and we can go back and live just like we used to." I was not as confident as I tried to sound.

Chopper seemed to reconsider. "One of my paws hurts. I don't want to walk far."

Boulder couldn't seem to stay still. "Well, where are we going to go?"

"Why don't we go a few miles into the mountains? It's safe there."

Boulder snarled. "Oh, great idea! What are we going to eat in the mountains?"

"How about ptarmigan?"

"You'll never catch one." Chopper shook his head. "They're too fast."

"I have caught them before and I can catch them again. Come on, let's go. I'll show you both how to hunt ptarmigan."

We spent the next two days in the foothills, and my pride took a beating. We found nothing, not even a squirrel.

Eventually, we came back to the only place where we could find the simple life that we seemed not only to crave but to need.

We were cautious. We stuck to our routine of hiding in the day and feeding at night. Everything was going well until one evening when we arrived at the dump, only to find smoke in the air. Our beloved stink pile was on fire.

We looked on in bewilderment. Why would these stupid humans want to light this great pile of food on fire?

Boulder was the first to approach the blaze. We could smell meat burning at the edge of the flames. It was just out of our reach, but Boulder couldn't help himself. He slouched down as low as possible and inched his face closer. I could feel the heat, and could imagine how hot it felt on Boulder's muzzle. Boulder's lips and teeth were just about to bite down when a lick of flame lashed at his face. Boulder jumped backwards, his lower lip pulsing, and he rolled on his back, growling in pain and embarrassment.

We did not eat that night, and for the next five days the dump was enveloped by flames, the hot piles of our beloved garbage smoldering out of reach.

We all looked skinny and beaten. We needed to find another way to survive.

Chopper said that he knew where we could find food. He'd once broken into a cabin a few miles out of town, and he claimed that he could show us how to rip apart the door, promising that we'd dine like kings. I told them that the plan sounded pretty dangerous and reminded them that if we were caught, the flash of a smoke pole could be our last sight.

In the end, we all agreed that if we were careful, we could outsmart the humans.

We arrived at the cabin the next afternoon. The first thing I smelled was the latrine. I would never understand why humans chose to empty their bowels in exactly the same place every time. No other creature did this. Humans seemed to be detached from the most fundamental of nature's rules.

It was not the biggest of places, and in some ways it reminded me of a beaver dam. Chopper circled and sniffed all around the cabin. He honed in on one corner, squeezed one claw into a gap in the wood, and began to pry at the planks.

Boulder and I stood guard. It was quiet, and other than the strange caribou antlers that stuck out from the cabin's roof, high willows and trembling aspens were all that surrounded the building.

There was a loud grunt. Chopper had got the door open.

Once we were in, we made ourselves comfortable. Cans were clawed open, and bags of dog food and dried salmon were discovered and promptly consumed. Suffice to say, we enjoyed every minute of our stay in this fantastic place.

That evening, Boulder found a warm spot up on the bunk, and Chopper and I lazed on the floor. We decided that this cabin was a great place to spend the rest of the summer. Boulder said that he knew of a lake nearby where there were twenty more that we could ravage.

I awoke the next morning. Looking around, I discovered that I was the only one awake. I found a small pile of dog food we had missed the day before and some scraps of dried salmon. Surveying the cabin, I realized one thing was clear: three grizzlies in a cabin sure can make a mess.

I heard the first boom as I lazily munched on the leftovers, and the sound startled me more than the time Tikka pushed my face into a cold river. Mother was right; humans were very cunning. I hadn't even noticed them approaching. I knew I had to fight or run, and my first instinct was to run.

Boulder charged headlong out the front door. One of the humans trained his smoke pole on Boulder, and it barked again. By the human's exclamation, it seemed he had missed his target. He turned his attention and his smoke pole to me and Chopper. He and the other human began slowly approaching.

Chopper growled deeply and popped his lower jaw in a warning, but they continued to move closer. The big bear's fangs were in full view in the doorway, and his eyes were narrowed in a vicious slant. I could tell Chopper was both angry and scared. He wasn't going to run. He was going to fight.

He growled again, and the sound sent one of the humans bolting down the road. Chopper lowered his head and charged out of the cabin door. The remaining human stood firm. His smoke pole spat fire.

Chopper surged onward. The human fumbled with the smoke pole and ran for the only cover nearby. He was still several feet from the outhouse and Chopper was closing in fast.

To this day, I've never seen a stranger sight. Chopper chased the human round and round the outhouse, in turn gaining ground and falling behind, sliding wide of the tight corners. The human shrieked and took every corner like a gopher on a blueberry. This went on for some time.

Boulder and I stood transfixed by this incredible spectacle. Was there anything as undignified as a human? They were truly out of place in our world.

A smoke pole sounded again. Chopper's shoulder dropped and he rolled, but within seconds he was back on his feet. His eyes were wild, his fur matted with blood. All he could focus on was killing.

When the smoke pole exploded outwards, Chopper was only a few feet away. I remember the image of the human's smoke pole actually touching Chopper's face when the next shot rang out.

Chopper cried out only once. Then, silence.

"We have to go," I told Boulder, shouldering his flank. But Boulder just stared at Chopper's body, half-hidden in the long golden grass. He turned away from me, and walked out into the sunlight. The human turned to watch his approach, his smoke pole raised. The timid, playful Boulder I'd known had disappeared. His eyes had glazed over, the pupils fixed on the human clutching the still-smoking pole. Screaming horribly, Boulder hurled himself forward.

There was a loud, metallic click.

The human stumbled, his eyes wide. He hurled his smoke pole at Boulder, and scrambled back towards the trees.

I called out again to Boulder, but he didn't seem to hear me. Moving in closer, I realized that I too was ready to fight. The human kept yelling and waving frantically at us, but I felt a quiet rage well up inside of me. I could taste his fear on my tongue....

The human scrambled into the trees just off of the dirt road, and we both slowed. We knew he had no escape. Without pause, we split up and circled the human through the pines.

Boulder made his final charge. I loped in closer.

The human had made it halfway up a tree. Boulder was at the trunk, tearing at his heels. I ran to help, watching Boulder try to rip the human down while the human shrieked and pulled himself higher into the branches.

All of a sudden, Boulder fell back. He righted himself and spat out a dark, fleshy lump. It was the heel of the human's boot. The little man, crying now, shimmied higher into the tree.

Boulder's guttural grow surged into the tall lodge pole pine, and white froth dripped from his lower lip. Standing, he scraped deep claw marks into the grey bark. Pine cones began to fall all around us as the desperate human wheezed and screamed out for help.

Boulder and I stood at the base of the tree, peering into the branches. The human was just out of reach.

Minutes passed. We circled below, growling and talking about Chopper, our anger growing. I stood up again and pushed at the base of the tree. Boulder joined me and soon the long, thin pine began to sway, and as the branches clashed together, clouds of pollen poured down upon us.

Boulder sniffed at the air, ready to catch this tree's trembling squirrel when it fell. But although the tree swayed violently as we pushed, the human didn't budge, having wrapped himself tightly around the trunk, his red eyes bulging from their sockets. The standoff continued.

With Boulder guarding the tree, I headed off to check on Chopper. I soon found him. He was motionless in the grass, his fur twisted and sticky. I shook him on the shoulder. "Get up! Get up!" I clawed and bit down along his neck trying to rouse him, sniffing at the red hole where the smoke pole had punctured his flesh. I growled at a horsefly that lapped at the moisture around Chopper's eyes. A few white clouds drifted in silence overhead as I realized my leader was gone.

When I returned, Boulder was digging at the roots of the tree.

"What are you doing?" I asked.

"If I need to, I'll rip up the entire forest to kill this beast."

I didn't respond straight away. "We have to go. The humans will come back with many more smoke poles. Killing this human won't bring Chopper back."

Boulder hissed something unintelligible, and continued to tear at the tree's roots.

"Boulder, please, we've got to leave. I'm begging you. Let's move. Let's travel far away from here."

Boulder stood firm. "This place is my home. It's the only place I know."

I sighed, and reached out to touch his arm. "There is a huge world out there for us. We can be something more. We can be more than just garbage dump grizzlies."

He didn't look back. "I'm sorry, Rumble Bear, but I'm okay with this life. You know, we're not all cut out to be wild grizzlies."

"Well, I'm not staying here. It's too dangerous. Finish your business here and I'll meet you back at the dump in a day or two."

"Okay."

I walked slowly back into the cover of the bush. I was about a mile from the cabin when I heard three shots echo down the lake. I rose and listened, straining to hear a roar or growl, but a final shot rang out.

I knew right away.

Boulder was gone.

CHAPTER EIGHT

When A Grizzly Is Ready, A Master Will Appear

I was alone again. I knew that the dump was too dangerous, and with Boulder and Chopper gone, there was nothing to go back to. So it was into the wild again for me, and I was full of apprehension and doubt as to what my fate might hold.

The stillness and silence of the bush eased my mind a little, and as the days grew longer and the memories of roads, trucks, dogs, people, and smoke poles faded, some of the stress that seemed to constantly travel with me floated away.

I was on my seventh day without any meat. Although hunger was burning in me, I noticed that my condition seemed to be improving. I moved faster and slept more deeply, and my senses seemed to heighten with each day.

After feeding on berry patches up in the alpine bowls, I decided to journey in the direction of the far end of a lake that I often caught scent of on windier days. As I descended, I noticed many more well-worn game trails branching out in every direction, and the myriad smells and tastes on the wind seemed to widen in variety.

I enjoyed walking through the shale and sand towards the lake. The ground began to steepen. Feeling good, I rolled and tumbled playfully downward. Sometimes the mountains provided me with natural, gravelly slides. As I leapt, dropping from one small ledge to the next, I unexpectedly broke through some soft ground and began skidding over a bank. This was no longer just a steep hill. A glance over the ledge I was quickly approaching showed me that I was far higher up than I'd thought. Scrambling, twisting, I grabbed at twigs, rocks, bushes—anything to slow my fall. It was no use. As I slipped, my claws searched desperately for traction. They finally caught just as my body was almost entirely over the edge that led to a straight drop. I glanced down and saw a narrow ledge a few feet below where my feet where dangling. I closed my eyes, slipped off, and whump! I landed on my rear end, and sat in a daze for a few moments catching my breath.

I gave one good head-shake, trying to paw the dust from my eyes. Blinking, I looked up. I was sharing this narrow ledge with the biggest, meanest-looking grizzly bear I had ever seen. I could actually hear my heart beating in my ears like a woodpecker.

I sat in total silence, trying to think what to do. I shifted slowly, glancing over the edge to scout out any escape routes, but there was nothing. As I turned, the sleeping giant awoke. I froze. He blinked rapidly and yawned, rolling out his huge neck and shoulders. Then he saw me. In a second, his face changed completely. He curled his lip and growled low and deep.

As in most nightmares, things got worse. As he slowly rose, he seemed to grow bigger and meaner by the moment.

I could tell that he was aggravated by my intrusion. I knew what would happen next. It was simple: I was going to die right here on this ledge.

I tried to back up carefully, but all I ended up doing was emptying my bowels all over the rocks. I heard a purring, submissive cry slip out of my mouth. I pushed my head flat to the ground, doing my best to show how small and weak I was. I most definitely posed no threat to him.

He sneered. "Scram, little bear! This is no place for you."

I pulled myself backwards along the shelf, trying to get as far from this grizzly as I could without slipping over the edge. He stood there watching me slink backwards like a weasel. The anger had faded from his face. Now he wore an expression of pity and contempt.

He growled deeply and shook his head. "What a pathetic bear." He lowered himself back down and closed his eyes to continue his nap on the sun-soaked rocks.

It was as if I was unworthy of notice. It was as if I was a mole or mouse. I continued to crouch, watching for any movement on his part. Soon, he began to snore.

It was only then that I noticed his face was matted with dried blood. One of his claws was missing, and his breathing seemed labored. This bear had recently been in battle. The more I looked, the more scars I saw. He was one of the oldest bears I had ever seen.

The old bear groaned, twitched, yawned, and opened his eyes again.

"You're hurt."

He grunted. "Get lost, little bear. Listen to your fears and run far away from here."

"What is your name?" I stuttered.

"Leave me now. I'm weary from battle, but I assure you that if you continue to bother me, I will drive you off this ledge the hard way."

"Is there some way I can help you?"

"What could you do for me?"

"Are you hungry?"

"Yes. Bring me a nice fat rabbit and I promise I won't make you my next meal."

Now, a rabbit is no easy animal to hunt. Their huge ears constantly swivel, searching for potential enemies, and their reflexes are faster than almost anything else in the bush. Finding and catching a rabbit was going to be one tough challenge.

Rabbits are unbeatable in the open grasses and are quicker than even gophers and squirrels among rocks and stumps, but they do have one weakness: they hate any kind of water.

I came up with a plan. Rabbits were abundant this season, and I remember Mother telling me that the cycles in nature seemed to follow a simple rule of boom and bust. She explained that when the wolves, lynx, cougars, and bobcats are at their peak and seem to be everywhere, a bear should travel higher into the mountains. Nature seemed to know a correction was needed, and she would soon cast her spell of change.

I wanted so badly to show this grizzly that I was not pathetic. I believed my luck would improve if I again had a friend in this harsh world, so I crept quietly towards the lake shore, tiny rabbit trails appearing beneath me. The first rabbit I saw disappeared underneath a thick tangle of roots. I stalked more slowly. I could smell the creatures, and as I continued, I noticed seven or eight feeding in the grasses along the shore.

The wind was in my face and I pressed my body down into a stretch of soft moss. "Patience," I said to myself over and over. "Patience."

The shoreline dropped quickly into the lake, and from my vantage point I could see all the way across the deep blue water. I continued to watch the rabbits eat. They were content to focus all their attention on feeding. Only one rabbit's ears were raised, scanning for predators. One plump fellow's ears lay flat along his back and he spent much of the time in a light sleep, only occasionally waking for a brief look around. This rabbit would be my prize. This would be my triumph.

The wind grew stronger and the trees heaved. Branches moaned against the stiff lake breeze. The time was now—I would drive this rabbit into my jaws or into the lake.

My crawl started slowly. Even when one rabbit heard me and thumped a warning, my rabbit remained blissfully unaware of what was descending upon him. The ground was soft enough to muffle my approach. When I was only feet away, my prey jumped, his legs twitching for traction. I sprang forward, trying to sink my teeth into him, but life is often a matter of inches and I missed my target.

I had fully committed, and as I drove my body into my attack, the rabbit bounced off of my chest, splashing into the lake. I leapt in after him, sending up a huge splash. When my head popped to the surface, I saw the rabbit swimming desperately for shore.

This was my last chance. I swam hard and fast, and with one quick swipe of my paw, the juicy, fat rabbit was on the menu.

As I climbed the bank, I tried to convince myself that the old grizzly had demanded only half a rabbit. No. I knew that my own hunger was now almost out of control, but some part of me wanted to show the old bear that he had been wrong. I was not pathetic and yes, I was actually a good hunter.

When I got back, I saw that the old bear had moved to the far end of his little ledge. I stopped and gazed out over his high rocky perch. I realized how smart this location was. It gave him clear line of sight to anything that approached. I decided to quietly climb along the trail and place the rabbit where we had last spoken. I dropped the limp rabbit on top of a round rock. I liked how it made the rabbit seem a little bigger.

The old bear didn't move, so I decided to fall back a short distance so that when he awoke, he would know that the food was my offering and not something we needed to fight about.

I lay down on the sandy rocks. I was tired and hungry, and soon I too had nodded off in the warm summer afternoon.

Crunch! Crunch! I looked up. There were rabbit guts all over the old bear's face, and bones cracked as he ate. I watched as he stripped the meat from the fur. It looked delicious. I wondered if he might leave anything for me. A few more gulps and I had my answer.

"So, little bear. I think I shall call you Rabbit. That seems to be your only talent."

"No, I have also taken beaver and ptarmigan," I blurted.

He laughed "Yes. I'm sure you have. But have you ever sunk your face into a thousand pounds of moose and eaten for days until your gut damn near dragged over the rocks when you walked?"

"No," I answered quietly.

"What do you call yourself?"

"My name is Rumble Bear."

He paused and cocked his head. "And just who gave you that name?"

"My mother. She said that my name came from a great grizzly bloodline, and that someday I would walk amongst the great grizzlies of the world."

The old bear laughed out loud. "Well, your mother, I see, told you some great fables. I can see by your stride and build that you might have some grizzly in you, but I can assure you that you're a lot closer to a rabbit than anything called a grizzly."

I felt anger well up, but what could I do? This huge bear was more than I would ever want to tangle with. I tried to change the subject. "What name was given to you?"

"My name is Stikine, and I just might be the first real grizzly you've ever met."

This was my chance to gain a little respect. "No, I've battled like you. I also carry scars."

Stikine scanned me from top to bottom. He nodded. "I see someone has hung a good licking on that ear of yours."

"Yes. I fought a bear in the marsh flats named Tobaldi."

The old warrior looked me straight in the eyes. "Do not lie to me. You don't possess that kind of courage."

"But I did." I told him about the times with my mother and about what had happened to me when I went looking for her. I also told him about my life with Boulder and Chopper in the dump.

By the time I had finished, I realized that Stikine had fallen asleep. It was twilight and as darkness arrived, I waited for him to move or hunt, but he lay still as death.

I curled up and waited for what might come in the morning.

CHAPTER NINE

It's Not What You Say but How You Say It

"I need a drink." These were Stikine's first words to me that morning. He lumbered down the shale slide, and I followed. I noticed that he favored his right shoulder. His pace was steady, and when a new meadow or opening appeared, he never stopped to listen for danger. He would occasionally pause to smell the wind, but this was only for hunting. He seemed fearless. Danger was no concern to him.

When we dipped our faces into the cold lake, the water was clean and the freshness shook us awake. When bears get hungry, we almost enter a kind of trance. Nahani once told me that this was one of Mother Nature's motivational tools, and the only solution was good grub. For the rest of the day we foraged on tubers, stink nettle, and grasses. We spoke little, and Stikine seemed to almost forget I was there.

I eventually broke the silence. "Have you ever been to the marsh flats?"

"Sure, many times."

I had spent only one day there and almost lost my life. I could only imagine what must have happened to Stikine there.

"Have you ever fought a bear as strong as Tobaldi?" I ventured.

"In my prime, a bear like Tobaldi would have been afraid to drink from a stream in the same valley I occupied."

I snorted. "This bear is going goofy," I thought, but his growl wiped the smile from my face.

I quietly followed Stikine into a shadowed valley. "Where are we going?"

He didn't look at me. "To the caribou hills."

Hours later, Stikine circled a small patch of mountain pine trees that grew around a large black boulder with white veins of quartz running throughout. In the distance I noticed a single dark cloud drifting our way. We knew a burst of summer rain was coming, so we each tucked into the green limbs and bedded down. The rain soon began falling in earnest, and we listened to the water as it ran off the rocks. The rain clouds danced in the alpine winds, and soon enough the wetness eased. I stood to shake the moisture from my fur. As I did, I noticed a big shadow breaking in the sky. My eyes caught something large move past.

A huge golden eagle was perched on the black boulder. He tilted his head to one side and stood, peering down at us.

"Stikine," I whispered, "there's a golden eagle above you."

He didn't look up. "I know."

The eagle stayed on the rock all night. The next morning, as I stretched, it watched me, standing perfectly still, ever vigilant.

"Stikine, look at the size of that eagle. He is absolutely beautiful!"

"Yes, little bear, I know him well. He has been my companion for many seasons. He comes to me more often with every passing year."

"You have an eagle that follows you?"

"Yes. Many of the great grizzlies I've known have told me that they too are followed by golden eagles. Over the years, I have left meat many times as offerings for my eagle. He watches, watching over me, as my destiny unfolds."

It became cooler as we climbed, and we passed small boulders and washes of sand and gravel. I loved how Mother Nature composed her art. She could paint marvels with just time and melting snow, and her curves and contours were always perfect.

Eventually we stopped and wedged ourselves into a grassy knoll. From this high up, we could see the entire alpine expanse.

Stikine warned me that we would only be successful if I did exactly what I was told. The first lesson I had to learn was to quiet my mind so that my body would be ready for whatever may come.

We sat absolutely still for one full day and night. As dawn broke, I simply could not stand it any longer. "Let's move. This is so boring." Stikine pulled his lips back to expose his teeth and raised his nose to the wind. I caught it too: mountain caribou.

We both lay like brown stumps in the little patch of grass. The wind was perfect, and within minutes, the caribou were all around us. They fed in short bursts, scanning their surroundings in a continuous dance of foraging and watching.

Soon there were three, then five, and then a dozen. This was more game than I had ever seen in one place. Stikine sat at the ready without so much as a twitch. He turned his head to look behind us, and I saw grey antlers just on the other side of our little depression. Stikine started to move slowly towards the velvety antlers. Every time he placed his paw down, he paused to make sure no twig or rock would give his advantage away. I stayed perfectly still and watched him perform his dance of death.

One thing has been proven time and time again: over a short distance, a grizzly has few equals. Stikine pinned the startled bull caribou and bit down so hard on the back of its neck that the kill was instant.

I stood back and watched Stikine feed. It wasn't until half a day later that he finally wandered off to drink and I could at last taste caribou flesh. This was bear heaven. It was my first meat in so long that I fed in total rapture for hours.

I awoke some time later, my muzzle still wet with blood and saliva. I must have dozed off after gorging for so long. One reason a grizzly should always bury his kill is that the scent of blood can travel many miles on the wind, wafting straight to the nostrils of another predator.

In the distance, Eleven-Thirty raised his nose to the wind and closed his eyes. He knew by the smell that either something small was dead nearby, or even better, something large a bit farther off. In his commanding tenor, three sharp howls called out to his pack. Like distant thunder, a single howl echoed through the valley. Then another. Soon the whole valley rang with the calls of the Snake River wolf pack, and Eleven-Thirty waited restlessly for his soldiers to arrive.

The wolves, driven by the smell of meat, were closing in fast. Wolves can cover ground at a pace few other creatures can match, and I have always had a healthy respect for their endurance. No one wolf can match a grizzly, but when these forest ghosts gather, they are a force to be reckoned with—fast, cunning, and deadly.

My full stomach and the warm sun had made me careless, and I lazed about on the ground, unaware of the pack now quietly surrounding me. A faint sound stirred me from sleep. I saw a flash of black in the trees. I sniffed at the air.

Mother used to warn me that wolves were tactical fighters. They can't match a grizzly's raw power, but they are masters of confusion. They attack and retreat, using their speed to wear out a larger opponent. A well-placed wolf's bite can cripple and even kill a grizzly.

All at once, they were upon me. A sea of grey fur swept from the trees. Teeth and claws glittered in the sun. I barely had time to roll to my feet before the first wolf pounced, teeth groping at my arm. I lashed out, sending the beast flying. More approached, biting at my legs and backside, and I spun round, claws flailing. But it was like fighting the wind—they were always just out of reach. I retreated, backing off towards a rocky outcrop, and managed to cover my back. At least they couldn't get around me now. I roared, and spit frothed from my lips. I knew if I could hold them off, Stikine would soon arrive.

It was a stand-off. As the alpha male, Eleven-Thirty was first on the unattended kill. He ate quickly, tearing at one hindquarter until finally he was able to twist it right off. Some of the other wolves piled on, snapping at the caribou, but the rest of the pack kept me pinned to the rocks. White fangs and short howls met my angry stares. I turned in time to see a wolf smash into the cliff-face behind me. Following its trajectory, I saw Stikine emerge from the trees, his face a furious grimace. Eleven-Thirty was the first of the wolves to turn. He bared his fangs, but even he was not interested in this fight. He ripped the hindquarters from the corpse and vanished into the undergrowth, his pack scattering. Stikine stood over his kill and spread his huge arms across the carcass. This was his.

The wolves had disappeared as suddenly as they had arrived.

It had taken no time for the wolves to take a great deal of our prize. Stikine said nothing, but I could tell he was angry with me for not protecting our hard-earned caribou.

"Wolves," he muttered. "That's why when I get the chance, I kill any wolf I can."

"I hate Eleven-Thirty too," I said. "He's always out there waiting and lurking ever since he attacked Mother and me at our den."

I didn't say it, but I was really afraid of him.

"Well that's the thing about wolves. They only attack weak, sick, or old bears."

"Did you notice that not one of those wolves stood to fight when I arrived? I see that they had you penned in like a porcupine, frothing like a fool as they ate from your kill. You have a long way to go on your journey, little bear. You must become a better fighter. When wolves enter your space, they must respect your power."

CHAPTER TEN

The Porcupine and the Moose

Under the midnight sun, Stikine and I bedded down to rest, the bold black wolf still fresh in my mind. As I closed my eyes, I thought of Mother and remembered her final tale of the winter wolves.

Eleven-Thirty sat in the middle of his pack, scraping away the last few pieces of the caribou. He looked up to find his pack staring hungrily at him and at the large glistening white bone before him.

His full winter pack was made up of over forty wolves, but autumn was still in the air and only seven of his strongest wolves travelled with him now. As the leader, he knew any sign of weakness or hesitation would bring a flood of challengers. His years as alpha wolf had made him cold-hearted and shrewd. One of the largest wolves in his pack was a broad-shouldered gray wolf named Tiberius, a brave hunter and important pack member. But last winter, Eleven-Thirty had noticed Tiberius making long glances at some of the females.

The large caribou bone was packed with tasty marrow, and a fully-grown wolf like Tiberius could crack open the treat in moments.

A white-and-grey peppered female, Sankaa, eyed the large bone as well, saliva dripping from her lips.

Eleven-Thirty turned to walk away, knowing the scramble for the precious white bone would start as soon as he left. Tiberius, the strongest and biggest, arrived first—a little too soon—and Eleven-Thirty spun to viciously tear at Tiberius's mane.

A loud yelp broke the frenzy, and with an air of disdain, Eleven-Thirty turned his back to the pack and reached down to collect his bone. The wolves whimpered in fear and stepped back as Eleven-Thirty sauntered towards Sankaa.

He dropped the bone at her feet and held the entire pack back, waiting for the perfect moment to allow her to feed. When he gave Sankaa an acknowledging roll of his head, she crunched into the bone. Tiberius made no sound, but his eyes burned.

It took more than just brute strength to become the alpha male. Eleven-Thirty had learned over the years that fighting was a dangerous game that had broken, bruised, and even destroyed many of the great alphas. He had learned that manipulation and domination were far more effective tools.

He ruled his pack like a benevolent dictator, always pushing and pulling at the other wolves' emotions. He never felt more alive than when his pack surrendered to his total dominance.

Back when he was a pup, Eleven-Thirty would often venture away from the den. Sometimes all the commotion caused by his sisters, brothers, and aunties was too much and he'd need just a few moments of peace and quiet. He could still remember the day he'd met that stranger, the lone wolf who'd relied on his cunning to survive.

He remembered hearing of lone wolves, and knew that they were not common. The Snake River pack patrolled their borders for just these kinds of intruders. This lone wolf was cautious and seemed relieved to find that Eleven-Thirty had seen fewer than two seasons.

"Just passing through, kiddo. No need to tell Mommy. Okay?"

"I won't tell," Eleven-Thirty said.

"Good. You're a smart wolf. You look unusual—all black with just a slash of white, I see."

"Yup, that's how they made me," Eleven-Thirty responded, a little flattered. "What pack are you from?"

"Well, originally from the Bonnie Plume pack, but there was a little…situation. I had to leave."

"Leave? Why?"

"Well, I'll be frank. It actually had to run for my life."

"What did you do?"

"Well, let's just say that a very pretty little wolf named Nova made it extremely hard to follow all those rules we wolves seem to love so much."

Eleven-Thirty nodded slowly, though he didn't quite understand.

The elder wolf continued. "I myself enjoy a bit more of a bohemian lifestyle. You see, kiddo, rules are like the taste of grass. Common and just plain boring."

"But the rules make the pack stronger, right?" Eleven-Thirty ventured.

"Yes, I guess so, but who really benefits from a strong wolf pack? Take a moment and really think about that, kiddo."

"Well, I guess the alpha male benefits the most."

"Bingo, little buddy." The lone wolf chuckled. "It's always those guys. They seem born to win it all."

"Yes, but they fight and hunt for the pack. They should get something."

"Sure, but how much is the question. Nobody ever dares to ask. I remember my pack's alpha. He always ate first, slept first, his dens were the deepest and driest, and all his females were constantly ready to serve his every want. You know, looking back, my little friend, I can't ever remember my pack leader's ribs ever being broken or his face kicked when taking down all those tough winter moose. Yet it always seemed perfectly natural that he alone should take the very best parts for himself."

Eleven-Thirty thought about this. He had a point. That happened in his pack, too.

The loner paused, cocked his ears toward the den, then looked back and continued. "But you know, kiddo, there is one thing I truly did learn: some things are really off limits."

The loner's eyes sparkled with life and a big grin appeared. "But you know what, kiddo? She was worth every bit of it."

Eleven-Thirty could tell that this loner liked a little company and was hungry for conversation.

"Has anyone ever told you the secret story about the porcupine and the moose?"

"No," said Eleven-Thirty.

"Oh, well, it's one of my very favorite stories in the whole world." Eleven-Thirty looked back towards his den, but no one seemed to have noticed his absence. He moved in closer to hear this windswept wolf's intriguing story.

"Well, the story goes that many years ago, an unusually bitter winter rolled in, with deep snows that coated the land. The cold was so savage that many creatures suffered the winter ear-bite. Their exposed ears froze so badly that they simply broke off like dried leaves and tumbled away into the snow."

"Wow!" Eleven-Thirty blurted. "Why didn't the animals just dig out some kind of den for shelter during the long cold nights?"

The loner chuckled. "Well, I've never seen a moose dig a den. Have you?"

The legend goes that a very old porcupine was trudging in the deep snow when a young moose almost stepped right onto his back. The moose scraped away some of the snow and ice from around the little beast. "Hey, old fella," he said. "What are you doing travelling in the deep white? Aren't you supposed to be in a tree well or perched under some branches somewhere?'

"Yes, that sounds like a fine place to be," the porcupine said.

"Well, why are you out here travelling in the scrub? There is no food out here for you."

"Just travelling through to the next forest over," said the porcupine as he patted down some of the snow around him. "It is nice to see the sky again after tunneling along in the snow for so long."

He was a very old wise porcupine who had been lucky enough to have seen a great deal of Mother Nature's secrets. He looked up to study the young bull moose. "Ah, young and strong, full of life, you must travel with great ease with those long legs of yours. Nothing can catch you in even the deepest snows." The porcupine smiled.

The proud little bull held his head high. "Yes, that's right," he said.

The porcupine told him, "I've been lucky in my life to have had three very different moose as friends. They say that all moose fall into three types, and I have had the good fortune to be friends with all of them. I wonder which type you are?" The porcupine looked the moose up and down. "The first moose I met was young, fast, and strong. Like you, he thought little of danger and relied on his endless energy to see him through life's challenges. I remember we met along a wide winter lake, and the young moose wanted to cross to the better feed on the other side. But that winter produced only a few light snowfalls that just covered the ice. I remember that the lake was covered in crisscrossing wolf tracks which branched out across the snow."

The porcupine explained that this would be a very dangerous crossing for any creature, but without any concern, the young moose broke into a trot across the frozen lake. As he listened to the porcupine's tale, the young bull shook off some of the falling snow accumulating along his shoulders. "What a foolish moose he was," he declared. "I would not have taken that unnecessary risk just for a little more feed."

The old porcupine shook his head. "Who knows? The second moose I knew was in his prime, a huge bull with intimidating horns. He lived for his females, and his whole life revolved around those autumn days when the rut was at its height. All spring and summer, he fed on the best greens he could find, growing his huge fighting rack until finally his velvet horns began to itch night and day. This drove him to scrape them in a small stand of trees, peeling away the silvery grey membrane. One day, in the middle of the fall rut," the porcupine continued, "I was about to cross the narrows between two lakes when my old friend appeared. His eyes were bloodshot, and he had not eaten in a long time. We spoke briefly, for the calls and crashing of antlers at the far end of the lake were like a battle drum thumping in his head."

"Sorry to leave you now, porcupine, but I must go and fight these intruders."

"Fight them for what?"

"Well, for the females!" he said.

"But don't you have all the females you could ever want at this end of the lake?"

The enormous bull paused, looking at the old porcupine as if he were stupid. He pronounced, "There's never enough," and galloped towards the horn-clashing in the distance.

Hearing this story, the young moose said, "What a greedy, arrogant moose he was. If I had what he had, I certainly wouldn't have done what he did."

The old porcupine looked up at him and quietly asked, "Who knows?"

The tale continued. "Only a few short seasons ago, I spent some time with my last moose friend. He was an older bull, no longer fit for fighting, with silver hair growing along his mane. His fall rack, although still proud, was no longer the biggest in the land.

"He now spent more time alone, and food was his real joy now for he knew exactly where the finest water lilies and longest grass thrived. He ate well and grew his thick winter coat to prepare for the most challenging time of the year for his kind. The winter and the wolves were his only foes now. The old moose and I had met along a gravel road just outside a small town that sprung from the thick bush. Winter always meant a lot of digging for the old moose, and he told me that this year he planned to go into town and rest and eat amongst the humans as they would clear the snow from around their homes and gardens.

"I told the old moose that there were many dangers in the town's fast machines and dogs, and that humans were to be avoided. But he said that he wanted to do something a little different this year, so off he wandered into town."

Listening to this tale with rapt attention, the young moose lifted his head, looked around for any danger, and turned back to the porcupine. "Well, these are some very unique moose you've known. Again, I would not have been so foolish as to walk willingly into a town full of humans. As you know, they can't be trusted."

The porcupine smiled. "Well, who knows?"

So whatever happened to these three moose friends of yours?" the young bull wondered.

The old-timer porcupine looked up at the young moose. "They are all gone now. You see, the young moose who trotted across the lake was one of only a few moose who made it through that particularly bad winter. He survived because he was the only moose on the far side of the lake, and the wolf packs, thinking no moose would have risked crossing the lake, only hunted on the western side of the valley that year.

"The moose who went to fight intruders was lucky because as he reached the far end of the lake, a big metal bird dropped off human hunters who stalked the far end of his lake for over a week. His decision saved his proud horns from being mounted on a wall in some faraway place.

"The grey-bearded moose who walked into town happened to find a very large backyard full of horses who were happy to share the hay and grains their humans brought daily. I understand it was one of his most comfortable winters yet."

And with that, the old porcupine told the young moose that it was time to move on. "I hope we meet again, moose. We porcupines know that if you meet a young moose, you should take the time to say hello because it's not often in life you make three friends in one."

Young Eleven-Thirty laughed. "You mean that was all the same moose, but in different stages of life? That's a crazy story!" The wolf barked with joy.

The lone wolf sensed some change in the air. "Got to go, kiddo."

Eleven-Thirty wanted his new friend to stay. "Will I see you again?" he asked.

As the lone wolf slinked into the trees, he howled his answer over his shoulder. "Who knows?"

CHAPTER ELEVEN

Why Fear Follows Us All

For the next few weeks, Stikine and I stayed in the mountains. We followed the caribou as they grazed in the lush bowls and side hills of this special place. We made two more kills, and I spent hours watching Stikine, trying to learn his art of hunting big game.

I saw that strategy was every bit as important as speed and power. I learned the cycles of our prey: when they feed, when they watered, and where and when they would rest.

We used every advantage we could. I remember Stikine's lesson that surprise was our greatest weapon. On our last hunt of the summer, Stikine stalked the caribou herd from upwind. He wanted them to focus on his smell and sounds as he moved in the bush.

I was kill-bear for this hunt and I didn't want to disappoint my teacher. I also didn't want to disappoint myself.

As I lay in wait in the low brush, a nervous mother and calf appeared in front of me. Their attention was on Stikine, whose scent led them closer and closer…

I had just let go of the calf's neck when Stikine appeared. I backed away from the fresh kill as I knew that around fresh meat it was simply best to let Stikine feast in peace. I secretly hoped that he would forget the calf's fatty pink tongue which drooped on the pebbles. He didn't. The ripping of hide and the occasional crunching of bone made my empty stomach growl even louder.

When snow hits the high country, all animals, including us bears, start our descent. I had learned so much by watching this great grizzly. Stikine would rarely reminisce about his past, and he never gave thought to the future. I realized that what made him so at ease was that he lived entirely in the present, only concerning himself with what was happening right now. The fear of what could happen next never entered his mind.

This gave Stikine something that I desperately sought. I wanted it more than anything. I wanted to live without fear.

One night, we settled in along a small creek trickling its last water before the winter freeze. The last light started to fade, and I saw the great golden eagle land and take his vigilant watch over us.

"Stikine, what is the eagle's name?"

"His name is Nechako. Some grizzlies say an eagle is a bad omen, and that it brings death, but I don't see it that way. I know that he is here as my spirit guide, and that when my final moment arrives, I will not be alone. I know that he will take my soul high into the mountains and that my death song will echo through the valleys and lakes."

"Don't you fear death, Stikine? Don't you worry about your death?"

"No. I think only a grizzly whose heart is filled with regret fears death."

"Stikine, how did you learn to live without fear?"

"Little bear, I have felt fear often. When I was run off by my mother, I had to endure many hardships, but one thing seemed true. Every time I was afraid, every time something terrorized my thoughts and sickened my mind—when I walked towards that fear and confronted what scared me, the same thing always happened."

"What? What happened?"

"I gained confidence. Whenever I was courageous, my confidence grew, and the power held by things that seemed so terrible would weaken and eventually die."

"But surely there are things we must fear, Stikine, like humans, other bears, starvation."

"I agree that we must be aware of them, but to fear them is foolish. You see, thinking about what might happen tomorrow or next year is of no value. It is much better to be clear of mind and live your life now so that all the decisions you make will be for the right reason and not because something might or might not happen."

All night I thought about what Stikine said. Next morning, as we enjoyed our first drink of the day, I turned to the older bear. "Next season, I plan to walk the world without fear like you do."

He chuckled, gazing up towards the golden eagle gliding the thermals above. "The reason little bears don't become grizzlies is because they always plan to be what they want to be next season. Remember that one day your golden eagle will quietly appear, taking his place as your constant companion until he takes your spirit, flies high and proud, and screams your death song to the world."

Just then, a tremendous crack of thunder shot down the valley. I flinched at the sound's suddenness, as the sky was bright and no dark clouds were anywhere to be seen. Again an awesome crackle pulsed out from the mountains. Stikine chuckled. "That's not from the sky, little bear. That's the great white rams fighting in the cliffs."

I had never seen goats or Dall sheep, but I remembered Mother telling us about these creatures and how they lived almost all of their lives on the tops of the highest mountains in the world.

Stikine stood on his hind legs, pointed his ears towards the mountains and smiled when the thunder of horns clashing rumbled into his waiting ears.

Stikine sat down in some soft white lichen, rolled onto his back, and rubbed his shoulders, scratching away happily as the sun warmed his belly.

"You know, Rumble Bear, Dall sheep are really amazing. When I was young, I was one of the only grizzly bears ever to go into the high country and hunt the great white sheep. They are magnificent to watch. They are completely at home standing on cliffs where not even Nechako would dare perch. Even the little ones can scamper and jump like you wouldn't believe. Their little hooves stick to almost everything.

"And let me tell you, Rumble Bear—although they may be smaller than most deer, in my expert opinion they are the best-tasting creature Mother Nature has ever created." Stikine's eyes had misted over. He was staring into the mountains, a smile on his face. He turned to look at me.

"Their eyes are so strong that if you approach from the open meadows below, they'll disappear and may not return for days.

"I remember one hunt in particular. I was way up in the mountains, so high that the snow never melted, not even on the warmest summer day. The only weakness I ever found in the mountain sheep was that the Dalls always concentrated on looking down the mountain but rarely ever looked above. They just assumed nothing could climb higher or more quietly than one of their own."

Stikine itched his belly a little and ground his shoulders against the earth. "I remember getting to the very top of this one particular mountain. I was certain that any goats or sheep on the other side would, by now, be three mountains over. I had dislodged so many rocks and boulders that crashed and tumbled down behind me that I thought this was turning into more of an adventure than a hunt.

"But when I peered over the crest of the mountain, to my total surprise only twenty feet below me were two white Dall sheep on a rocky ledge. I was so close I could smell their breath. They had beautiful snow-white fur and golden-brown horns. I always think of those creatures as noble. Their white faces and black noses make them look quite distinguished.

"But, Rumble, what is really impressive are their horns. From the top of their heads grow thick, sweeping battle horns, with bony ridges spread along each one. Some say that every season Mother Nature grants them another ridge to honor another year lived in her mountains."

I moved a little closer to Stikine. He was never usually this talkative, and I didn't want to miss a word of the old bear's tale.

"Did you jump down and get them both?" I blurted.

"No! Relax, little bear. You always want to get to the blood and gore. That's not what this story is about."

I dropped down, resting my chin on the cool tundra moss, and listened.

"You see, the wind was perfect. I could stick my whole head and shoulders over the peak to look down at these two rams. I could see the shadow of one of my ears along the backside of the younger ram.

"I almost ruined my hunt right there and then, but I slipped back a little and calmed myself, trying to think what I should do next. I was so close that I could even hear them talking. The younger ram was upset that he had lost a fight, and was telling the older ram how this was so terrible and that he would never have a chance to mate and that everything was over for him."

Stikine looked at me and chuckled. "Sound familiar, little buddy?"

He continued. "I remember vividly what that old ram said. I guess all those years in the mountains had taught him a few things about life."

If those two rams had only known what was stalking them from above! Rumble held his tongue, but was bursting to hear about Stikine jumping from the very top of a mountain to take the two sheep down.

"I can still remember the old ram's deep voice. He said, 'Oh my. That sounds terrible. You lost a fight against a stronger ram. This could be life-ending. Maybe you should banish yourself and live with those smelly mountain goats on some cold dark mountain somewhere else.'

"The young ram didn't really appreciate this advice and was a little taken aback by the old ram's lack of empathy. One of the tips of the older ram's horn had broken off, and his eyes were a little bloodshot—probably from years of hard winters. He asked, 'You see that lake way down below?'

"The younger ram answered, 'Yes, I can see it.'

"The elder ram continued on, recalling a time many years earlier when the spring and summer were cool. The sheep had to travel down to that lake for their water every day until the rains fell again. As I heard him tell the story, the journey was fine at first, but soon a single wolf noticed their travels, and then a black bear, and soon after, a very big grizzly. They had all waited along spots on the trails, hoping for a sheep to stumble. Over those few weeks, the herd lost some of its old and some of its very young, but they carried on their journeys.

"Then, Rumble, the old ram tilted his head, looked down the mountain, and said, 'Do you see that blonde grassy area just yonder?'

"The young ram slowly answered, 'Yes, I see it.'

"Then the old ram remembered back to a warm windless day when two spring ewes jumped and played on that very spot, both full of life and enjoying the comfort and safety of the high peaks. 'Then, a long shadow fell across the grass and two large talons dropped from the sky. A golden eagle plucked one of the ewes and then dove into the valley below.' The younger ram began to pace behind the older ram. His problems seemed a little less important. In the distance, a clash of horns turned the old ram's head, and he stood up and looked down on his world. Crack!

"'Oh, how I love that sound,' the old ram bristled. 'When two equally matched rams meet, it is the one with the most courage that always wins.'

"The young ram was now filled with a new, uncomfortable feeling: regret. 'Maybe I ran a little too soon from the fight,' he admitted. 'But when my horns crashed into that other big ram, he hit so hard that for a few moments my eyes couldn't focus and it felt like my brain would never work again.'

"Rumble, the old ram was angry now! 'That's not how the gods made you!' he shouted. 'You have all the tools to win. You couldn't even begin to imagine how many times I stood dazed in front of a ram, but I was always ready to fight on. Win or lose, it didn't matter to me. I was in the game and I would play all my pieces. I only wish that I could be young again. I would do everything exactly the same. I have not a single regret.'

"The old ram lifted his head high and faced the younger ram. 'No more whining. No more feeling sorry for yourself. Here's your simple choice. You're a young, strong, healthy Dall sheep. Either you show up for life, or you go and hide somewhere. It's completely your choice.'

"Then the old ram stumbled as he stepped along the grey rocks on the rocky cliff. He placed his next step carefully and felt for some firmer ground. And Rumble, you won't believe what happened next!"

I was hanging on Stikine's every word.

He continued, "As I looked down on the two sheep, the younger ram noticed my movement. When he realized what I was, he was so frightened that he exploded into one powerful bounce and disappeared from the ledge. I stood up on the very peak of that mountain and looked down, knowing the old ram would, in the next flash, be gone forever."

"The old ram looked right at me. We both stood completely still for what seemed like minutes. I remember my mouth starting to moisten in anticipation. Then the old ram called out, 'Who's there?'

"I didn't say anything. 'Who's out there?' he called, and he waited, straining, listening for a reply.

"As you can imagine, Rumble, there was something a little off about this old-timer. But I decided to approach. I had just placed my first few steps when, of all things, the old ram started to walk deliberately, rock by rock, towards me. I couldn't believe my luck. With each moment, he came closer and closer."

Seemingly in anticipation of the climax of Stikine's story, Nechako landed with a whoosh, tucking his wings back to rest for a while. He hopped closer to Stikine.

"Well, there stood the white ram only a few feet from my very face. You know, I can confidently venture that never ever in all of Mother Nature's entire history has she ever seen a big grizzly and a Dall sheep standing face to face on the peak of one of her mighty mountains.

"I mean, what a sight to see! When that old ram finally caught my wind, his head slumped just a little with the realization of what he had just walked into. There was nowhere to run, and he just braced himself for what he knew was coming."

My excitement grew as I listened. I stood up on my hind legs, imagining myself and the white ram on the mountain. I smashed my paws into the tundra and growled like I was Stikine and like I had just vanquished the wise old ram. Then I blurted out, "And with only one swipe of your mighty paw, you removed his head and it bounced all the way down the mountain—right?"

Nechako and Stikine looked at each other like disappointed parents. I was suddenly embarrassed. "Ahh…sorry about that. I was just kidding around. Ummm…go ahead and finish the story."

Stikine rubbed his claws along the white lichen and continued. "Ah no, little bear, that's not what happened. You see, when I looked carefully into the face of that ram, I could see a cloudy film covered his eyes. He was completely blind. He travelled the cliffs and ridges of those mountains purely from memory. If you can believe it, we just stood there for I don't know how long. Finally, in a deep, strong voice the white ram said, 'May I pass?'

"Not knowing what to do, I said, 'Do you know what I am?'

"The afternoon winds were now starting to swirl around us. The ram said clearly, 'Yes, you're a grizzly bear.'

"I stepped closer, only inches now from the ram's weathered face. The mountain grew quiet. Still the ram said not a word. 'Yes, you may pass.'

"The proud old ram exhaled and his shoulders relaxed. Tentatively, he took a step forward and his face brushed along my shoulder. He paused, took a deep breath, adjusted his direction and slowly walked towards the steep slope I had scrambled up many hours ago. I turned to face him and shouted out, 'I liked your story, old ram.'

"He turned back and answered, 'Well, I don't think I've told my best story yet.'"

I couldn't take anymore. "What? You let him go?"

Stikine smiled. "Yes, I let him pass."

I stood on my hind legs. "You let him pass! You should have let him pass through your stomach!"

Nechako and Stikine howled with laughter. I smiled, placed my claws like a set of horns above my ears and stumbled around, pretending to be the old blind ram in the mountains. Bobbing my head, I said in my best woodpecker voice, "Can I pass? Can I pass?"

CHAPTER TWELVE

FINDING THE TRUTH IN THE HOT SPRING

Dawn's light washed over my face. I could hear that Stikine was extra cranky this morning. His old body seemed to delight in me reminding him of his long and reckless life. "I need my medicine," he called out. I walked over to him.

"Ya! Some fresh moose marrow or calf heart would be fine medicine—no, wait a minute," he grumbled. "What I really need is to soak these old bones of mine."

"Soak?" I asked.

"I need the hot spring!" he shouted, and without another word he rolled over and started towards the trail. I hurried up behind him.

It was early fall, and we were well fed. We would both cruise easily into hibernation with a few more good feeds. I had heard of hot springs before, but no one had shown me these secret places. Not missing what I didn't know, I was quite happy to live my life without ever seeing one.

By midday we had travelled down into what appeared to be a ravine. The only giveaway that it might be somehow different was a slight smell of sulfur that grew stronger with every step.

Ahead, I heard a huge splash and a burp-like groan as Stikine flopped into a small hole.

I looked down into the pool. Only the very top of Stikine's head and his bright smiling eyes showed through the misty steam that bubbled away in this amazing place.

I watched as Stikine played and enjoyed himself. It was like the waters had made him young again. I placed my paw on top of the water, but the heat was so great I pulled away quickly. The rocks seemed to hiss in the cold air as if they were angry we had found them. "Get in, you little rabbit bear!" Stikine called. He was so different in this place; it was like his spirit had become young and playful again.

I stood on my back legs and peered into the hissing pool. I caught Stikine's raised eyebrows, and, grinning, I dove in.

The heat coursed through me immediately, warming every bone in my body. With our hair soaked and matted to our faces, Stikine and I floated for hours, enjoying Mother Nature's pain medicine. "Stikine!" I yelled. "Why did you keep this a secret? I love this place!"

"I didn't know if I liked you enough to show you my hot springs."

Having spent the better part of a day in this soothing heat, neither of us was interested in walking into the fall night soaked to the skin. Instead, we stayed and talked among the white wisps of steam. I won't forget our conversation for as long as I live.

It started simply enough. I think I asked Stikine about the toughest beast he'd ever faced.

He dipped his face into the pool and then rolled his neck back and rested it on the ground at the water's edge. "That's an easy question. The toughest creature I ever met was a wolverine."

I laughed as I watched the steam battle the cold air above. "A wolverine is no match for a grizzly bear."

Stikine turned slowly to look at me. "Of course, but have you ever come across a furious, cornered wolverine?"

"Well...no."

The older bear's eyes seemed to mist over in the steam. "Many years ago, I made a kill in late fall. I can't remember what I killed, but I can remember every line and scar on that old wolverine's face. After I made the kill, I circled the area to mark my domain. To my amazement, when I returned to my hard-earned feast, there, eating my favorite part—the liver—was an old wolverine.

"Naturally, I was furious. I roared at this brazen thief, but the little terror didn't even look up from the kill."

"Woohoo! Here comes a beating." I laughed.

Stikine pawed at his nose. "You would think so. But that old wolverine, when he finally acknowledged me, looked me dead in the eyes and growled his dominance over my meat."

"Tell me you split that little bandit into a hundred pieces."

"No, I didn't."

"What?" I stared open-mouthed at Stikine. "Why not?"

"You see, in all my years, nothing that small had ever had the courage to stand face-to-face with me. I knew that if I wanted to, I could kill this wolverine, but there was something more important than meat happening at that moment. What I realized was at that very time and place, I was a witness to something special.

"For the next few hours, I watched this amazing creature fill his belly in the most dangerous situations nature can provide. Nothing comes between a fresh kill and a grand grizzly bear. But watching that little warrior tear at my meat, I learned three important truths."

Stikine had my full attention. My soul had searched for these important words and I knew I was ready for the answers.

"First, I noticed the obvious. Yes, the wolverine was only one-eighth of my size, but his sheer guts were ten times those of any bear I knew. He faced me and ate his fill on the knife-edge of death with his gods of war behind him. I knew he was game to fight me at the first twitch of my attack. His attitude never changed. At his core, he simply knew that he was tougher than me.

"The second lesson I learned that day was that even something that small could command his body to release all its power without fear. You see, as I watched that wolverine eat my kill, both he and I felt a dreadful tension rising. I knew that he could recognize the anger in my eyes, but every so often, at the perfect moment, he would stop, hiss at me, and roll his neck and shoulders almost as if he was pushing the fear right out of his body. Like a pup, I watched in a trance, wondering if I too could push all of my fears out of my soul, leaving only what really mattered, leaving only the real me."

This story was almost too crazy to believe, but Stikine's voice had never been clearer, and the hot springs seemed like a near-sacred place where only the truth could be spoken. With his eyes now closed, Stikine delivered the third important lesson.

"After over two hours, the wolverine ripped away a huge piece of the underbelly and slowly backed away from the carcass. He was now twenty feet from me. He dropped the bloody meat and looked me right in the eye, and at that moment I realized that this standoff had not been his first. The sly, confident grin spread over his face as he backed away, his unique salute to my submission. It seemed to say that he looked forward to feeding on my next kill." Stikine fell silent.

"Did you ever see him again?"

"No. But I never forgot that wolverine's attitude and courage. Those sorts of guts can be found only when someone has pushed himself over the edge time and time again."

Minutes passed as we soaked our bodies in the quiet of the night.

"We'll need to get out and walk off this wet before the coldest part of the night arrives," Stikine said.

"Stikine..." I asked in my calmest voice. "Would you show me—"

He cut me off. "Yes! I think, little bear, that you have never felt the real grizzly inside of you. Tonight that all changes."

Stikine swam closer to me and stood facing me, the water lapping around his neck. "Tonight you will push out the fear and let the real Rumble Bear roar. When we climb out of this pool, I want to hear a growl so fierce that it sets every beast in this valley trembling with fear. Understand?"

"Yes."

"This is your one shot, Rumble."

I climbed the bank in silence.

Stikine screamed, "NOW!"

I roared as loud as I could. It was pathetic.

"Again!"

I roared louder this time, and Stikine grew madder. His disgust stung me deeply.

"Rumble Bear, you roar *now*."

I pushed my lungs and threw my battle cry into the heavens.

"Yes!" screamed Stikine. "More!"

I pushed out all the fears in my chest. My roar became deeper and louder than I had ever hoped it would.

In pure joy, Stikine began roaring, and together we stood on our hind legs reaching for the moon above, roaring in sheer grizzliness, enjoying every breath of this moment. We roared louder than even Mother Nature's thunder, pushing out all the burdens, regrets, and pains we carried with us. We bellowed like lords of the night, reveling in the sheer joy of living.

CHAPTER THIRTEEN

WOLVES IN THE WILLOWS

Stikine and I eventually made our way to the far end of one of the many lakes in his vast territory. He told me of char, fish similar to the great salmon that spawned in the rivers to the west. Thoughts of these fat and juicy fish spurred us on, and soon enough we reached a shallow plateau in the lake. Following Stikine's lead, I rolled some of the boulders on the lake's bank, and Stikine arranged them so that the bright silver creatures had no other choice but to swim by our fish-drunk fangs and claws.

We were both fat, and our winter hair was thick and warm. I had never felt so strong in all of my life, and I often thought of that lazy, stupid, fearful life I had lived at the dump.

Very soon, I knew, we would both wander off to den up for our long winter sleeps.

Stikine said he would soon leave me. He could feel hibernation taking hold. He complained that his teeth were bothering him and his eyes and ears were only half what they once were, but he said that next spring he wanted to see the grizzly flats once again.

I felt cold dread at the thought of Tobaldi. "No way. Not me. I'm not going there. What on earth do you want to do in that terrible place?"

Stikine chuckled. “I like to watch all the bears cowering near the flats, trying to pretend that they’re grizzlies.”

“Why do you want to watch that?”

“Because every once in a long while, I get to see something rare.”

I was completely confused. “What’s that?”

Stikine looked intently into my eyes. “I get to see courage.”

Over the next few days, Stikine would wander off into the brush every now and then with a char in his mouth. I could smell the fish on the breeze and meandered over towards the smell. To my surprise, Stikine had created a small pile of uneaten fish. Some were rotting and the smell was growing more potent with each passing hour.

Eventually the run of fish disappeared from the lake and Stikine summoned me to him. “Little bear, I have something to do. You guard our pile of char.”

“How long will you be gone?”

“I don’t know. It depends on you.”

I was puzzled. “On me? What do you mean?”

“You, little bear, have something to do. Just remember, what you think of yourself will eventually become true.”

Stikine was losing his mind. I sometimes wondered if he would survive another season.

Just before he slipped out of sight, he turned and growled. “Fight like a grizzly.”

Two days passed and the pile of rotten char was starting to smell like bear candy. I lay and waited for Stikine's return. The snowline was almost to the lake now, and I was ready for a long, peaceful sleep.

At midday, my eyes caught movement far off along the lakeshore. I rose and sniffed the air, but I sensed nothing. Then, off in the distance to my right, I heard a long, powerful howl, and moments later another.

I was instantly alert and my muscles were locked and ready. Wolves. I hated them. Surely Stikine had heard them too, and he would soon appear. If they wanted a fight, I knew he would give it to them.

I dragged the pile of fish into the tall willows and waited for what might appear. It was not fear I felt but anger, and this made my thoughts clear.

I growled deeply. I felt the cold moss beneath my paws and the wolves' scent drifted into my nose. I felt ready for any wolf who wanted to challenge me.

Eleven-Thirty skulked from the shadows up ahead. Like half-seen ghosts blurring into focus, four wolves appeared behind him. They looked hungry, and their yellow eyes darted to the pile of fish scattered at my feet.

The hair on my shoulders stood up straight, and my eyes burned as they approached. I was no longer afraid. I felt calm and alert, and it was not a matter of if but when we would battle.

The only thing left to decide was which wolf would die first between my jaws.

The wolves moved less surely than they had when I'd last fought them. They sniffed at the wind and kept their distance, their growls low and tense. It seemed as if they'd expected a different bear.

They formed a circle around me and began to howl. Eleven-Thirty fixed his eyes on mine, and I realized that I no longer saw him as the great black killer wolf I'd once been so afraid of. He was just another wolf—and he was no match for a grizzly—a grizzly like me.

He trotted back and forth through the willows, confined to the space between the branches. The hunger in the air grew stronger. More and more wolves emerged from the darkness, yellow eyes igniting in every corner of my vision. I breathed steadily, singling out my first target: Eleven-Thirty.

The first bite hit me on my haunch. I twisted round, claws singing, but the wolves at my front darted in to distract me. Pain shot through my rump again, and I spun to meet the challenge.

It was Eleven-Thirty. He darted in to tear at my leg. Bolder now, the wolves moved in closer. The fish piled at my feet were being smashed into a sort of slimy mud which intensified the wolves' feeding frenzy even more. White fangs and piercing eyes glittered everywhere.

Then came the attack. On my left side, a large grey wolf lunged for my underbelly, and I smashed his head with one powerful swipe. He instantly rolled away, yelping in pain. His defeat seemed to frighten the others—all but the almost-midnight-black wolf.

He growled, and soon he and I were the only two left in the willows. He howled for reinforcements and I knew the pack would soon return, but for now my only focus was this wolf. This was the one who had hunted me for so long. The one who had attacked my family. He would no longer haunt my thoughts.

We circled. He would not back down, but neither would I. Advancing, I pushed the growling wolf deeper into the willows, barring his escape. Eleven-Thirty's eyes began flickering back and forth, and he began to glance into the trees in the direction of his pack. Sensing victory, I readied my claws for the final battle.

I charged, swiping at his neck, but he slipped beneath my flailing paw and bit down on my chest. I pinned his back leg down and roared terribly. I could smell my blood in his fangs. He bit down harder, twisting the skin beneath my fur. That would be his greatest mistake. Raising both arms high, I pounded at Eleven-Thirty's spine and in his agony, his grip loosened.

He began squirming beneath me, trying to escape, but I was not finished yet. I drove my fangs onto his shoulder and tore backwards, flinging the black wolf into the air.

I felt no pain, nor fear. I saw only my enemy.

The pack had returned, but no wolf dared approach. They yelped and cried and howled as their master struggled, but it was all just noise.

My power was clear to all. We rolled and kicked and tore and slashed until I had my jaws round Eleven-Thirty's powerful neck. I shook him until there was a loud snap. The black carcass fell from my mouth, lying limp before me.

I stood with my front paws on the savaged corpse and roared in triumph.

The wolves seemed to have lost all interest in the fish pile. They ran with their heads low, their submissive yelps ringing out into the lake.

I knew that I would not see Stikine again until the spring, so after a few more bites of char I wandered a few miles from the lake and dug my winter den. I was suddenly terribly tired. The snow was deep and cold, but as I curled up for my long hibernation I felt only peace. So much had changed.

CHAPTER FOURTEEN

SAGE WORDS FROM A GOLDEN EAGLE

Spring arrived, and my den was now awash with the snow-blue crystals of a new season. I dug myself out, stretched, and surveyed my kingdom. I was lean and ravenous, but my wounds had healed well over the winter and I had hibernated deeply and peacefully.

My thoughts drifted to Stikine, and I wondered if he had fared as well as I had over the winter. I wanted to continue our adventures for at least one more wonderful season. I realized that it was he and he alone who opened the secret door into the world of grizzlies.

I promised myself that I would now live the rest of my days as a real grizzly.

I foraged the green shoots and grasses that grew along the lake for a few days, and life began to sprout all around me again. Soon the summer bounty would start. I was in my prime and ready for the world.

I waited and smelled the air, but no Stikine. I began to think of all the terrible things that might have happened to my old friend, but I pushed these thoughts away. On the third morning by the lake, I wandered down to the water's edge and leaned down to drink.

I closed my eyes and dipped my face into the water. I always liked this time of the day. The birds were quiet and the lack of wind made for a deep stillness that I found incredibly peaceful. As the water dripped from my chin, I looked down into the lake.

I saw Stikine's reflection.

I was so excited. I turned around to greet him, but no one was there. I stood up and looked again searching for my old friend, but nothing. I looked down again into the lake's reflection, and this time I saw something different.

What I was staring at was something almost inconceivable. I was staring into the eyes of a massive, powerful grizzly. My head and face had broadened, and my jaws and snout seemed like they were chiseled from stone. My shoulders and chest had grown thick and rippled with mature muscle. I stared at this new reflection and studied my battle scars. I felt a new feeling, one that I had never felt before. It was hard to explain, but I would describe it as a kind of steady calm.

I heard some branches snap and the unmistakable rumble of a grizzly moving in the brush. I let out a quick growl and waited for a response.

Nothing.

The sound grew louder and moved straight towards me. I prepared myself, for this lake was meant for no other bears.

This place was mine.

The sounds drew closer—the creature was moving quickly through the timber just above the shoreline. Then silence. I watched carefully for any movement. I glimpsed a flash of brown.

If this was trouble, I was ready.

Stikine sauntered out of the bush. "Where's my pile of char, little bear?"

I trotted over to see him up close.

He cuffed me playfully. "Looks like you had a good sleep. I see you finally put some muscle on that body. You know, if I wasn't so old and senile, I might even mistake you for a real grizzly."

"Look, old-timer, you'd better be a little nicer to me. I'll be the one making all the kills this season and your jokes might affect the amount of meat I'll grant you."

We laughed and enjoyed our time foraging for the new green shoots our bodies craved. The snows in the mountains were still too deep for travel, but I suggested to Stikine that we should go where a couple of grizzlies might find a feast.

Over the next few weeks, we wandered all over our territory. We managed to kill an old bull moose who was thin and weak from a long, tough winter. The meat wasn't as sweet as the young spring caribou, but we both gorged on the carcass and soon our hair and claws were sleek and sharp.

The golden eagle was now our constant companion and even perched on our kills. We always left the eyeballs for he seemed to delight in those gooey treats. One afternoon, Stikine wandered off for his afternoon nap and I was enjoying the spring sun on my back. I found some particularly soft, dry moss and spread out for my snooze.

I looked up to notice Nechako circling above. His wingspan was almost seven feet across, and his massive black talons spoke of his strength. He flew quietly, only occasionally pumping his powerful wings for altitude or for a course correction. He was majestic.

My eyes closed, and I fell into my favorite dream. It was always the same and began with Baja and me wading into a shallow river teeming with our favorite red sockeye salmon. The pools of fish were so thick that they almost jumped into our mouths.

"Thump! Thump!" The sound awoke me. A whoosh of air announced the arrival of Nechako.

"Hello, Rumble Bear."

This was the first time I had heard Nechako's voice. It was older and fuller than I had imagined. The details in his face and mosaic feathers gave him a regal air.

"Hello, Nechako. It has been most interesting watching you and Stikine together."

"Rumble, you must know that you have brought a lot of joy to that old warrior grizzly. His life has been watched by many golden eagles, and I'm proud that he chose me as his spirit guide."

"Well, Stikine has brought a great deal to my life too. Without him, my journey would have been stunted."

"Yes. Rumble, I think 'stunted' is the perfect word. Of course, most of my life has been spent soaring and watching. The height gives my kind an advantage over almost all other creatures. The advantage of perspective is our greatest gift."

"Do all golden eagles follow grizzly bears?" I asked.

"No. There are fewer than a hundred of us now. Time and circumstances have diminished both the grand grizzlies and the golden eagles of this world."

Nechako stared into the empty sky. "Rumble, I know Stikine talks very little of his past. His ability to live in the present has given him an advantage over almost every other bear I know. Until you arrived, I thought this trait might vanish from the grand grizzly bloodlines, but now I'm not so sure. However, I think you deserve to know the real story of your old friend Stikine."

"Please, tell me more," I urged.

"He, like many grizzlies, was cast out into the world in his third season when his mother chased him away. His fate was not yet written and a difficult test marked his journey's real beginning. He will never speak of it, but he lost almost everything early one morning when he ventured into the Yukon River. It was late summer, and he was desperate and hungry. He knew to stay away from the loud smelly humans and their yappy dogs and dirty fish camps. They were easy enough to avoid, but a few miles downriver he noticed two big wooden wheels spinning away in the current. The river was loud, but he could hear thrashing and splashing somewhere inside this contraption. As the baskets dipped rhythmically into the river, the wooden parts creaked under the current's power.

"Stikine stood watching as two big salmon twitched and rolled and then fell into a box. Intrigued, he paced back and forth on the beach while again and again, huge king salmon flopped into the box. He growled and clawed the beach sand. More salmon than he had ever seen were only thirty feet from shore.

"The current was swift, but he was a strong swimmer and knew from crossing other rivers that it was better to start further upstream to account for the current. One hundred yards upstream he entered the mighty Yukon.

"He swam straight for this wooden island. When he clamped down on the leading edge of the wooden raft, he was instantly sucked under the logs. The silty water blinded him, and when the basket bumped the back of his head, he lunged and pulled himself onto the fish wheel. He shook off the water and carefully made his way to the fish box. A swirling mass of salmon!

"Stikine howled with joy and devoured the entire box over the course of a day. What he loved about this log raft was that while he ate, new salmon kept falling into the box. It was his own bear heaven.

"The hum of a motor in the distance was his signal to disappear. With a resounding splash he jumped off the fish wheel and swam to shore. Needless to say, when the humans found a damaged, empty fish wheel, they reacted first with their usual fear and then their more dangerous lust for revenge.

"Stikine carefully watched all the excitement from the bushes. When the skiff touched shore, the humans scrambled onto the beach, looking and pointing at his tracks while their pathetic cabin dog yipped away its warnings. They milled about, stomping and yelling at each other, trying to find the courage to follow the grizzly tracks into the deep bush, but after only a few yards they fell back to walking up and down the beach, mad as horseflies.

"Stikine grinned from ear to ear and sauntered further into the thick bush.

"Two more fish wheels, this time raided in the quiet of twilight, and Stikine was now putting on enough fat for a happy hibernation. There were many humans now in the area, and the river hummed during the day with boats travelling up and down the river. Stikine was smart and knew that if he hid well, all the panicking animals and birds would not give his day-bed away.

"As daylight began to dwindle, his hunting ritual began as it always did: with a good stretch, a long drink, and a head-down trot to the river. As Stikine's shoulders pushed through the brush, he caught his first glimpse of the river and the coast seemed clear, so he ventured farther out. And then—boom! The thunder cracked again. Boom!"

"Dogs yelped and humans streamed into the bush. Stikine ran full speed, crashing through the bushes and zigzagging round the larger timber. The baying dogs were gaining on him. These were not the usual weak house-dogs he had seen before. These dogs had the pace and speed of the wolf, but were smaller and, as he found out, were tough, mean, and most importantly, absolutely loyal to their humans.

"The dogs were right behind Stikine, constantly barking out his position. Distancing himself from the smoke poles was his only chance. He ran for what seemed like many miles with the huskies howling out every turn he made.

"Boom! Another bullet smashed into the rocks at his feet. Stikine ran for his life. Cresting the mountain, he tore back into the brush again.

"After ten hours, the dogs were still fresh. The humans were miles behind, held up by some old forest fire deadfall. The huskies circled the great bear, calling to their masters for what surely would be Stikine's end.

"A faint, high-pitched whistle blew constantly in the distance. The huskies yelped and listened, but the humans were miles away. The dogs and Stikine were still moving, but they too were beginning to tire from the long chase.

"Stikine was desperate. 'Leave me, huskies. Let me live and I will not hunt near the Yukon again,' he pleaded. The huskies simply howled louder. 'Answer me, please! I will not bother the fish wheels again.'

"One lunging husky spoke up. 'Don't believe him! He's a grizzly! You know you can't trust anything these bears say.'

"The whistle sounded again, fainter, this time even farther away. 'We should head back,' another husky growled. Another disagreed. 'We can't! You know the salmon he ate were meant for us! Some of us will starve this season because of this buffoon.' At this, they all howled in anger. 'No! We stay and finish this bear.'

"At this, Stikine turned and stood his ground. The dogs circled and the standoff began.

"Stikine looked down at the raucous dogs. 'There are no humans here and no smoke poles. You know, I've always wanted to try husky.' The dogs continued to howl and bay, but they backed off a little.

"Stikine licked his lips and smiled. He charged at a tired female, just missing her front leg. The pack's will seemed to crumble, and a few of the dogs started back toward the humans. Those that remained backed further into the bush, growling at Stikine. The bear let out a wailing bellow, fangs flashing and teeth gnashing. There was a sudden stillness, when the last few huskies broke off and fled into the forest.

"Stikine marched into the mountains that night, expecting to never see the huskies again. He slept poorly, half-alert to the sounds of the forest around him. Snapping out of a groggy daze in the morning, he heard distant barks. He scrambled up, climbing the crest of the mountain. He could see the dogs some distance away, sniffing at the air. Two humans with smoke poles followed close behind.

"Stikine was in a full gallop. He fled down the backside of the mountain, making good time, all things considered. The sun was sinking in the sky when the first husky arrived on his tail, barking wildly and encouraging his companions to hurry. Stikine was in no mood for this battle.

"The dog snarled. 'It won't be a long day for you, I promise you that. Our two best hunters have one goal and trust me, they will succeed.' He howled with excitement as the other huskies arrived, madness dancing in their eyes.

"Stikine knew intimidation was not going to work this time. He pushed on, crossing a shallow creek, the dogs nipping at his haunches. He heard the first smoke pole blast in the distance. The bullet bounced away into the brush. Every time the smoke pole sounded, the huskies would retreat. They had often witnessed the power of the humans' weapons and they feared being caught in a crossfire.

"The chase lasted for the entire day. One of the strongest huskies was screaming at Stikine from behind. 'We will not stop! Our humans are prepared to hunt you to the ends of the Earth. They don't care how long you run. Soon even your strength will dwindle. Give up.' The inevitability of their success seemed to drive the dogs on.

"'He's done. He's done. I can see it in his eyes.'

"Another chimed in. 'Fish-stealing bear gets his dues tomorrow.' They laughed.

"Stikine ignored their taunts. 'I think I'll sleep right here. I look forward to eating you all tomorrow,' he chuckled, staring at the lead dog. Stikine turned his back and slipped into a dense thicket. The huskies, half-mad with rage, howled after him, but none were foolish enough to brave the thicket and almost-certain death.

"Once Stikine was deep in the heavy bush, he dropped to the ground in total fatigue. He had little energy left after days of being chased and harassed. As he rested, he thought about his options. Perhaps he could head back to the Yukon River. He could swim it again if he had to, and surely the huskies wouldn't follow, but he knew there would be boats all over the river. No, it was too dangerous for him to cross now. But where could he go? Another full day of running from the dogs would be just too much. He lay thinking, chasing the same thoughts round and round his head, searching for a solution. Soon the darkness would arrive. He knew he should cover as many miles as possible.

"The smell of smoke drifted in. The humans' campfire was much closer than he had guessed. These were strong, fit humans, not like those he had encountered before. He was surprised at their speed and stubbornness. Yes, these two men were different. The smoke carried the odor of human food—strong and salty.

"It grew darker now, and he dared to stand out on a nearby outcrop of rocks to survey the area. Way off in the distance, the campfire flames flickered. Stikine felt his anger rising. His hibernation was less than a month away and he knew the odds of digging his first den were getting worse with each passing hour.

"'Filthy, stinky, loud humans,' he growled. If they'd only not had smoke poles, he would have marched down there and throttled everything that moved. 'Weak little fools and their gutless huskies. At least wolves would show a little respect when they fought.' Stikine thought about the smoke poles. The thing about human weapons was that they had to be picked up and put away—and surely when the humans fell asleep the smoke poles would be safely out of reach.

"He pictured his attack. It would be unexpected, but he knew the dogs would bark their warning once they caught his scent. He stood still, thinking, watching the flickering flame in the distance. Could he finish this fight in the darkness? All the stories he had ever heard always ended with the same lesson: grizzlies should run from humans.

"But his circumstances seemed different. The inevitable chase that would come with the dawn would end with the crack of thunder and the huskies' happy howls. Stikine knew of no cabins in the area, so these two humans must be sleeping wild under the stars, just like him. The odds seemed in his favor—but there was still the issue of the dogs.

"During the day he had made note of each of the seven huskies. Four males and three females. Two were much bigger than the rest, but they were also much slower and had panted more than the others during the chase. They always seemed happiest when Stikine stopped to rest. Both would sleep deeply that night.

"A light rain started, and the wind grew a little stronger. Even the weather was on Stikine's side. 'A wet dog is an unhappy dog. But for grizzlies, a cold rain makes for some of the best hunting conditions.' Stikine began to plan out a strategy in his head. This could be his most memorable hunt to date.

“The rain came down in sheets. Stikine loved these storms—they muffled almost everything. He moved quietly, always checking wind direction, for he knew that a wet grizzly was a smelly grizzly. But Mother Nature was his friend tonight. He heard a tarp rattling in the wind up ahead. He was close. The smell of smoke was thick in the air, and he could smell the dogs. The fire crackled. He peered through the brush and saw the dogs huddled together, asleep beneath the largest tree. The tarp flapped loudly, but both dogs and humans slept on, unperturbed.

“The two humans were under the tarp, not too far from the campfire. Stikine watched carefully, looking for the terrible smoke poles, but everything around the fire looked out of place to him. He moved closer. Faint snoring was the only sound he could hear through the din of the rain. ‘One good head or neck bite,’ he thought, ‘will end this for certain.’

“He lunged while the humans slept. His claws swiped at the closest body, thick and spongy beneath the tarp. To his amazement, feathers exploded everywhere. He bit down again and again and the human’s cover just kept shooting out more feathers. The other human awoke to the shrill screams of his companion and he scrambled from his bed, half-screaming, half-crying. Stikine slammed a paw onto his leg to pin him down.

“The huskies yelped, tugging at their chains, trying to enter the fight. The human wriggled free from beneath Stikine’s paw and crawled for his smoke pole, but the bear hooked his thigh and sent him crashing into the fire.

“The human under the cover rolled into a ball, trying to play dead. Stikine bit into the flesh just under one of his arms, and the human began to scream anew. His flesh stunk, and his blood was strange and bitter.

“Two huskies had pulled their chains out of the ground and were biting at the grizzly’s belly. The other human had fled, his backside still smoking as he ran into the rainy night like a deranged deer. The dogs barked crazily, and Stikine clobbered one of them with a quick swing of his paw. The human under the cover lay rolled up in a whimpering ball as feathers floated like snow across the forest.

"Stikine considered quickly killing the whimpering human, but killing something he would never eat just seemed unnatural to him. Instead, he backed into the bush determined to cover as much ground as possible before daylight.

"At first light, Stikine turned his weary head and waited for the howls of the huskies and the sounds of smoke poles. They never came. He collapsed, his muscles burning, and sleep fell on him like the night's heavy rain."

I had been sitting this whole time, captivated. "Wow!" I said, "That is one wild story. So, Stikine has actually tasted human before and survived?"

"Yes." Nechako nodded. "That's when the first stories of Stikine started to drift into the mountains and valleys. The first time I ever flew over him, he was hunting mountain goat way up in the steepest ranges. Nothing hunted goats at that altitude, least of all grizzly bears, but there he was. To my amazement, days later I circled a kill and lo and behold, there was Stikine sleeping away, fat and happy.

"Two seasons passed before I saw him again. This time he was hunting caribou. He was a big, burly grizzly now, and I swooped closer to examine this fine bear. When I landed in a tree above him, I was surprised when, in a calm voice, he turned to look at me. 'I hope you're not here for me now, golden eagle.'

"'No, just resting,' I said. 'Do you mind?'

"'Well, you've already ruined my hunt, so go ahead.'

"I was taken aback. 'Sorry,' I told him, 'I guess to your prey, an eagle is a bad omen.'

"'Well, anything out of place will usually spook a caribou,' he said.

"'Will you hunt here for long?' I asked.

"'No. I'm heading to the marsh flats this season.'

"I remember looking down on him. 'Uh, the grizzly breeding flats. I've heard that they're very dangerous. Do you mind if I fly by when you arrive? I've never seen the place, but it sounds important. I would like to fly its sky someday.'

"Then he asked me my name, telling me, 'You watch out for me and I will do the same for you.' And that's how we met. On that day our fates were sealed. I was his golden eagle and he was soon to become my grand grizzly."

"Is that when Stikine fought Tobaldi?" I asked.

"No, Rumble. Tobaldi wasn't even born yet. Another grand grizzly named Growler ruled the flats. He had been king bear for six seasons. He was huge—the biggest grizzly I have ever seen."

"Even bigger than Stikine?"

"Yes, much bigger. He was a ruddy-colored bear, and he was famous for the huge tracks he left on the ground when he walked. Black bears, cougars, wolves, even the crazed wolverines would break into full gallop when they crossed his marks. He was so powerful that he went many seasons without even a single fight. He ruled the marsh flats like a grizzly general."

"Stikine told me that he lived on the flats for many seasons. Did he ever fight Growler?"

"Yes, many times."

I looked at Nechako with disbelief.

"You're not a grand grizzly if you don't rule the marsh flats," Nechako reminded me. "You know that. Stikine ruled the flats even longer than Growler. They say that he was one of the longest-ruling grand grizzlies ever."

My mind spun, thinking of all the time I had spent with this legend. Everything he taught me seemed to make sense now.

"When did he fight Growler?"

"He fought him that season, but it was more a wild chase than a fight. You see, Stikine is a tactician in almost everything he does. I told you about the human hunters and that rainy night because it was one of the many events that shaped him. He never rushes into anything dangerous without a realistic plan and some kind of advantage."

"That first fight was more of a test of cunning than anything else. Stikine approached and looked for some advantage, but the time was not right.

"The next season when I flew over, I could pick out Stikine easily amongst the other bears. He was even bigger than the year before. But Growler still ruled the roost, walking past all the other grizzlies into the paradise bowl to await his females.

"The second fight was much more intense. I remember much blood drawn that day, and it took Stikine's wounds weeks to heal. He travelled far into the mountains, and I followed him from high above. We spoke a few weeks later. Stikine was the lowest I had ever seen him. Like you, he thought he would never return to the breeding flats again. They were simply too dangerous for him.

"I thought for a few moments that this would be our last meeting. I sought only grand grizzlies to guide, not beaten whelps. Before I left, I asked him only one question: are you going to be a grizzly who walks towards his mountain or away from it?

"Stikine was tired. His wounds ached, and he was far from friendly. 'What mountain, Nechako, do you think I should be walking toward?' he asked me.

"I looked him dead in the eye. 'Your mountain, Stikine.'

"He told me that I was a crazy old bird, that no one creature could own a mountain. I sighed as only birds can. 'That's not what I'm saying. My question is simple. Are you going to follow your dreams, or are you going to stop walking and let them die?'

"He was incredulous as ever. 'What does that have to do with mountains, Nechako?'

"You grizzly bears really need everything explained! I told him that if I'd learned anything in all my years, it was that it may be easier to fly fat and happy in the lowlands than to soar in the dangerous turbulence of mountain passes. But the lowlands are for the weak of spirit; dreams live only on the very tops of mountains. We must choose to attempt the mountain. We should rejoice that our amazing journey is still possible, no matter what the final outcome.

"Stikine looked at me then. 'Thank you, Nechako, my old friend. Thank you. Yes, I'm still walking towards my mountain.'"

"So when did he fight Growler?" I asked eagerly.

"That's not my story to tell, Rumble Bear. That story should be told by someone who was there."

I jumped up and trotted towards Stikine in the distance. I could no longer mask my curiosity. "Stikine!" I called. "What happened with the bear called Growler?"

Stikine rolled back onto his rump and angled his ears towards me. I called out again. "Hey! What happened to that bear named Growler?"

Stikine rolled his eyes, visibly annoyed. He paused as I approached. "Well, let me guess. Did a little birdie tell you something?"

"Stikine, you have got to tell me that story. Please."

"Listen, bear, you have got to start making your own stories. Worry less about mine."

I shrugged, a little hurt. "Well, I don't have any stories like yours yet."

"I'm well aware of that. This is your season now, Rumble. It's time to forget everything that happened long ago. Find the courage to leave all of your suffering behind. Let it all fall from between your pads and wash away with your tracks as you travel the world as a real grizzly bear."

Stikine shook his mighty head. "Remember, Rumble Bear, what a grizzly bear thinks of himself is what will inevitably come true."

As we wandered, I noticed Stikine moved even more slowly this year and was unable to sight our prey as he once did. Thankfully his nose and his mind were still sharp.

One day as we stared out over a lake, Stikine began speaking without looking at me. "I want to see the marsh flats this spring."

I turned to Stikine, astonished. I knew I was not even nearly ready to face the marsh flats again. "No. No. Forget it. We have no business at the marsh flats this year."

"Oh, I think you'll have plenty of business at the flats this year, my friend," Stikine chuckled.

"Well, I'm not going to give Tobaldi a second chance at my hide quite yet, okay?"

"No, it's not okay. I see you don't fear the wolves any longer, but I refuse to travel with any grizzly who walks around scared all bloody day."

This was the first time he ever called me a grizzly. He'd always referred to me as Little Bear or just plain Bear. It felt good to be called a grizzly, but I was still unsettled over his stupid plan.

Stikine repeated his point. "I don't plan on living out my days with a full-grown male who's too frightened to explore his own territory."

I turned and tried to explain. "What you don't understand is that Tobaldi runs the flats. That is his place. He is the king grizzly and no one is looking for me to replace him."

Stikine stared right through me. "I agree. No one is looking for you. I guess you have to ask yourself if this is your time? Should you wait a minute longer to become what you really are?"

"Maybe I don't know what I am, but what I do know is that for the first time in my life, I'm living, breathing, and spending my days without fear. Why would I want to ruin that?"

Stikine coughed and shouldered past me. "This is only half of your life. You have not even attempted to make your real mark. Tobaldi is a challenge you must face before he robs those vital parts of you that can never come back. Remember, your eagle is soaring somewhere in the mountains, looking and preparing to guide you to your final moment."

I saw my opportunity. "Speaking of challenges, Stikine, what was your battle with Growler like?"

Stikine stopped on the spot, slowly raised his head, and smelled the breeze. "That old eagle circles for years, just watching, not so much as a word. But he gets around, Rumble Bear, and he's as chatty as a field mouse." He shook out his shoulders, rolled his head, and turned. "That was long ago and really shouldn't concern you, Rumble. Just leave the past alone. It's over."

"I think your story is exactly what I need! I won't enter the flats until you tell me everything."

"I think the truth is probably more than you can handle right now, Rumble Bear."

"I told you, I want the whole story. Stikine, speak the truth."

He sighed, peering into the canopy. "All right. I will tell this story once and then you will never speak of Growler ever again." Stikine's head swayed in a trance. "I had studied that arrogant bear for weeks, waiting and watching, looking for a weakness. My chance arrived when the swollen brute waded into the churning waters of the salmon river that morning. I chose that moment for two reasons: one, he would never expect my attack during the feeding frenzy of the red salmon run, and two, his huge size made him slow and cumbersome in the water."

"For three days I scouted the river, the ground, the boulders, and the lines of sight. I studied everything. I also pictured my victory and played the battle over and over again in my mind's eye. I knew where I would step, what angles gave me the best attack, everything I needed to do. I practiced holding my breath and I got comfortable biting and fighting underwater."

"I knew that morning's rains would swell the river, and a surge of new salmon would bring the king bear to the river's edge. When he arrived, every other grizzly vanished. Only he, the grizzly general, stood along the shore smelling for the arrival of his fish. I patiently watched from the bank behind him. From that vantage point, I still remember his massive silhouette. He looked like two bears wading side by side into the river.

"When I charged him that day, our battle was so fierce that I don't like to even speak of it. The river ran red, and the only reason I made it back to shore was because I, like Growler, was willing to fight until the end.

"The truth, Rumble, is that my story really should have ended that day. The odds of me ever killing Growler were small. I was prepared to risk everything that day. I knew that if I didn't succeed, my journey would end.

"And know, Rumble Bear, that you are in a similar situation. If you choose to follow me to the marsh flats this season, there is a good chance you may never leave those breeding grounds."

With that he strode on ahead.

I waited alone for a while. I noticed he never looked back. Nechako's question echoed through my mind. "Are you willing to walk toward your mountain?" I took my first step down the trail after Stikine. For the first time in several seasons, I felt the cold sting of fear.

CHAPTER FIFTEEN

If We Could Only See Ourselves Through Another Bear's Eyes

We were only a few miles from the marsh flats, and the smell of other grizzlies was everywhere. Stikine walked ahead of me, his huge graying head swaying in a constant rhythm with each step he took. Two large grizzlies walking together like this was very unusual, and when the first juvenile male grizzly caught sight of Stikine and me, he tore away, like a gopher looking for his hole.

Stikine stopped and carefully smelled the air for a few moments. I waited and watched as he moved off the trail and wandered into a small swamp packed thick with nettles and ferns. He looked back at me, growling. "Right where I remember them. I've waited a long time for this fermenting heaven. This is some of the best cabbage I've ever had."

I tried some. This swampy cabbage was tangy with a pungent aroma.

Stikine was still nosing the dark green cabbage. "This will be our home for a few days. I think it's a good place from which we can announce our arrival."

I was still terrified of Tobaldi, but with Stikine around I felt safe—the odds of Tobaldi fighting us both were slim. As dusk fell, I wandered back towards the main game trail. I was aware of my surroundings and unafraid. I knew Stikine was within earshot should anything happen.

With the wind in my face, I looked along the maze of game trails as they meandered in and out of the grasses and willows. My eye caught two bears approaching. It was a sow and her young cub. They stopped often, smelling, listening, and watching for any danger.

I lay down in the grass and waited. I knew a mother grizzly was nothing to take lightly, but it had been a long time since I had seen other bears and I was curious as to who they might be. I peeked my head out for a better view.

The sow saw me and instantly bluff-charged, placing herself between me and her cub. Her mouth frothed and she popped her jaws rapidly, warning me not to advance any farther. We remained like this, her neck stretched out, her legs braced.

There was something familiar about her. I looked closer.

Stikine emerged from the trees, moving towards her left flank. She backed away from us, visibly shaken by this second bear's appearance, but not once did she leave her cub's side. She let out a low growl.

I stepped towards her and looked more carefully. My eyes began to sing.

"Mother, it's me."

No response. She was far too agitated to listen. I growled to warn Stikine away and the female backed further into the trees, shielding her cub.

I tried again. "Mother, it's me. Your son."

As I moved closer, she growled, but it was softer now, quieter. Her expression slowly softened, and she cocked her head to one side, her eyes seeming to peer through me.

"Son? Rumble Bear?"

"Mother."

"Rumble Bear, I can't believe it's you. It's been so long—my, look how you've grown! And those claws. You look just like your father. I've been worried about you, Rumble—I'm so happy to see you're safe and well."

"I have missed you more than you will ever understand. Every time I hear the cluck of a willow ptarmigan, I always think of your face, Mother."

Nahani lowered her chin and rested it on her cub's back.

"I see you're a mother again."

"Yes, I think this might be my last cub. I have loved all my cubs. I hope they have all fared as well as you have."

Mother walked over and settled her cub between her front legs. "I heard that Tobaldi had killed you in a terrible fight. A female called Baja asked me many times about you, but it's been over a year since I've seen her. I don't know if she is still with us."

The cub peered tentatively out at me through wide eyes. Mother acknowledged Stikine for the first time. "I see you're travelling with another male."

"Yes, his name is Stikine."

She stared at me. "You travel with Stikine?"

"Yes. Do you know him?"

She paused. "Yes, I've heard of him. His reputation is well-known."

The wind changed directions and a familiar scent wafted in the air. Mother jolted backward before moving in closer. She lowered her head. "I'm proud of what you've become. I love you, and I will watch over you from afar."

With that, she turned and walked purposefully into the fading light. Her cub glanced back at me once more. I waved him on, and he scampered after his mother.

My heart was happy once again.

CHAPTER SIXTEEN

Wake Every Morning and Lovingly List Your Blessings

During our first night at the marsh flats, I slept little. The sounds and smells of other grizzlies in the area kept me on edge, but when I glanced over toward Stikine, he seemed totally uninterested in what any other bear was doing. He was lazing on his back in the grass, scratching at his belly absentmindedly. I smiled.

During the darkest part of that night, I heard Stikine moving, adjusting his bear bed. The bright full moon and twinkling stars always made me think that Mother Nature had been in a good mood during the preceding day, her enthusiasm spreading to her evening skies. Her divinity was perfection.

I wondered if I would see more nights like this or whether this would be my last.

Regret. That's what ate at me. Now, I was here in the sweet long grass, sleeping next to a bear who lived what I believed was a magical life.

"Stikine?"

"What? I'm trying to sleep."

"This is one of the best night skies I think I've ever seen."

"Yes. This one does seem extra special."

"Can I ask you one question?"

"Go ahead."

"What is the one thing in your whole long life that you regret?"

A few moments passed. "I wish that I had enjoyed my journey more."

"What do you mean? You're a legend! Your name is known all over this kingdom."

"Yes, but I remember Nechako asking me once what I would do when I reached the very top of my mountain. I told him I would stand and roar my battle cry so everyone and everything would see me. Nechako told me that he hoped that, when I finally reached the top of my mountain, it was because I'd always wanted to see rather than be seen.

"You see, Rumble, I wish I had enjoyed every step along the way, the good and the bad. Looking back, I lost too much time worrying about challengers, finding food, thinking about the next season and how I could keep and protect everything that I had fought for and earned.

"But those millions of moments were wasted. Now I am old, and my soul smiles at memories of the incredible female bears I loved, the way they moved and the energy and life they brought to me. I think back to my greatest battles and glorious hunts now and realize that when these moments happen in your life, you must remember to drink them in deep, to try and enjoy every single drop."

I realized that no bear could hope to enjoy every moment of their life. "When you were the grand grizzly for all those years, what did you think had happened to all those beaten challengers? What did life give them?"

"Yes, I thought often of those bears, and still do—where they are and how they're living. Only a few tried to take my kingdom more than once. Over time, I have come to respect those grizzlies even more."

"Yes, but you defeated them, so they were not really in your class."

Stikine shrugged. "But that's not how I look at it. All of my challengers had great courage, but when failure came, some just couldn't recover. Many never entered the flats again.

"Now I find that it is the grizzlies who carry their failures on their backs, who wear their losses with honor, that I consider both wise and strong."

"Yes, but if you carry all of your defeats around your neck, they're really nothing but weaknesses. I think it would be much better to hide my faults."

"On that, Rumble, you are so very wrong. If you think all of your mistakes and failures are things you should hide, I fear you will be the loneliest grizzly I've ever known.

"Failure only happens when a bear takes risks and tries to do something in the world. You must collect all of your failures, and I hope there will be many, and put them proudly on your back. You need to realize they are simply your payment to enter the arena. Scars, scraps, smoke poles, and a host of Eleven-Thirties waiting at the entrance of your winter dens—these things remind us that we are still alive and still walking up the mountain."

"Stikine, if I defeat Tobaldi tomorrow, how will I know what to do? How will I know how to live?"

He smiled. "First, change the question to 'When I defeat Tobaldi tomorrow.' For now, collect your thoughts for battle. And when this is all over, Rumble Bear, just remember that it's both a privilege and a burden to be a grand grizzly."

Dawn broke and our hunger pushed us into the flats. We roamed the tall grasses circling the area, sniffing the air for food. From a distance, we saw other male grizzlies, ranging from nervous cubs to larger bears in their prime. These bullish males were filled out, and sized up every grizzly who entered the flats.

The largest bears lingered around the entrance of the small trail leading into that magical paradise only Tobaldi dared tread. They were edgy, sensing the presence of the king close by.

Stikine and I strutted our way through the grassy flats and pushed the other bears aside. No one wanted any trouble from us. Stikine was at least as large as any other bear around, and I knew that I was just as powerful as he. My confidence grew.

I realized that the flats no longer felt foreign to me. Here, in this place, my power and spirit were welcoming me home.

Silence fell when Stikine and I stood at the entrance to Tobaldi's paradise. The other bears stood near, watching, not daring to speak. I could sense many females only a few hundred yards away. I looked at my old friend. "Let's both go. Together. Right now."

Stikine looked away. "Only one bear at a time can walk down that trail. Only a grizzly prepared to face anything and risk everything can reign supreme here."

"Why, Stikine, does this dark path make every part of me tremble? Many males have stood for long hours staring at this very entrance, and almost all have turned and walked away."

Stikine's eyes were lost in the tunnel's shade. "I know of the fear you speak. It is a wondrous thing. I have walked this trail thousands of times, and I used to love how just around the second curve, the canopy blocks out almost all of the sun's rays. I used to stop at that second curve, stand still for a moment, and enjoy the perfect canvas of terror that nature had painted."

He chuckled. "I even named it the 'Clinch and Gulp Corner.' It was almost like a living thing. It was as if a magical guard-wolf stood day and night as a grim warning to us male bears. That one corner has probably sent a thousand challengers back before a single growl was uttered."

I shuddered. "Why do you love this creepy trail so much? You talk like it's your old friend or something. You don't realize just how intimidating this place is!"

"Oh, I understand the power of this trail more than you will ever know. But if you move past your fear for a moment and think back to all the trails you have walked without any thought of what lay ahead, you will start to see that this trail is nothing more than a well-worn grizzly path to paradise. It's an old road that we've turned into a place of dread. In the darkest, deepest, scariest parts of our minds lie all the dreams and treasures we seek. When you're ready to walk down that path, stop at 'Clinch and Gulp Corner' and take a moment to see it for exactly what it is."

As Stikine finished, I felt my fur stand up on end, bristling outwards. Stikine was likewise ruffled, and I watched him squint as he peered deeper into the shadows. Tobaldi's acrid musk drifted into our noses. He was close by, and we both waited to see whether he would present himself. Long minutes passed as every bear in the area vanished into the thick ring of brush surrounding the marsh flats.

A low, powerful growl rumbled up from the trail. I could feel the blood rush through my ears. Moments passed and then, without warning or planning, Stikine and I simultaneously roared into the trees and willows before us. I was alive at that moment and I stood on my hind legs and roared again, even louder this time.

Silently we stood, waiting for a reply. Nothing. Stikine and I backed away into the tall grass.

I was confused. "Do you think he was afraid of us?"

Stikine smiled ruefully. "No. I don't think Tobaldi is afraid of us, but he is definitely aware of us now. He'll be wondering what kind of bear stands at his gates and roars at him like that. I think this advantage must be nurtured."

A good battle roar always makes me hungry for blueberries.

We spent the rest of the afternoon walking and feeding as we meandered up a side hill just north of the flats. The berries were small but sweet. From this vantage, Stikine looked down onto the flats. "When I ruled these flats, I often came up here to survey my kingdom."

I followed Stikine's gaze, peering down onto the wide plains. I could just about make out several females milling about in the sheltered bowl of Tobaldi's paradise. Then I saw him. Tobaldi was patrolling along the rim of his personal Eden. He seemed far less threatening from this distance, but I still felt his presence and his utter dominance, even from here.

Stikine watched with a longing look in his eyes. I sensed a certain happiness in him as if he was looking down on an old friend.

"Stikine, do you think Tobaldi ever feels fear?"

"I know for certain that he does."

"But how do you know?"

"Because I knew the great grizzly known as Smasher Bear and just how strong he really was."

"Do you think back in your day you could have beaten Tobaldi?" I ventured.

Stikine laughed, a sneer on his face. "In my prime, Tobaldi wouldn't dare sniff my droppings, let alone fight me. I've fought against bears several times bigger, stronger, and bolder than Tobaldi."

"But I don't understand," I sputtered. "Why is Tobaldi king grizzly?"

"In my last season here, the very fierce Smasher Bear and I battled over two days. Eventually my strength left me and I retreated. I almost died from my wounds, but I managed to survive hibernation that season, and Smasher ruled the marsh flats from then on."

Stikine's golden eagle flew in lazy circles above us. I watched his subtle dips and turns. He moved so effortlessly that his presence went unnoticed by the other bears in the area—all expect Tobaldi.

"If Smasher was the king grizzly, how did Tobaldi take that from him?"

"I heard later from an old bear that Smasher was so weakened from his battle with me that the next season, before Smasher's wounds could heal, Tobaldi challenged and killed the king."

I was quiet for a moment. "When you left the marsh flats, were you miserable?"

"Yes, for many weeks I felt no joy in anything. Life lost all its energy. I felt that I was finished. My best days were behind me. My place in the world seemed to have changed. Younger, stronger bears wanted to test their strength against me. I battled older, bitter bears who fought not for sows or food but for revenge. Those first days were the hardest, and I saw little joy on the horizon. But such is life. That too soon changed."

"But how?"

"You were the change. When you stumbled over that ledge, my new life began. You see, I needed you just as much as you needed me. Our travels were grand, and watching you change brought me immense happiness."

I moved in closer. "Thank you, Stikine. You have been a wise and patient teacher. It has been my honor to have lived and learned at your side."

Stikine glanced over the rich green flats. "Keep an eye down there tonight, for if you truly believe it's in you, you might just be living there tomorrow."

"But what if...?"

Stikine snorted. "Stop it! 'If' and 'maybe' and 'try' mean nothing. You will be ready when those words are of no use to you anymore."

CHAPTER SEVENTEEN

THE MARSH FLATS RUMBLE

I awoke to Stikine standing motionless above me. His eyes scanned the flats. I yawned as the morning came into focus. “What shall we eat this morning?”

“No food for you today, Rumble Bear. Just sip a little water this morning.”

I was hungry. “Why?” I blurted out.

“Why? Because a little hunger brings battle into our blood. I think I’ll spend my day doing something I relish.”

I realized that morning was probably the last chance I would ever get to ask Stikine any more questions. So I decided to ask him the one question that had been pulsing in my mind all night. “Stikine? What if I lose everything today? What if I die in battle down in the breeding bowl?”

Stikine held my eyes with his. “Yes, this could be your end today. But I ask you, Rumble Bear, if I could promise you the chance of a long life or a chance at an incredible life, which would you choose? You see, when I decided to battle Growler that day, I realized that it wasn’t how long my life would be that mattered. What mattered was how I lived and what kind of grizzly I became.

“I will sit here on this knoll today and watch from afar. Whether you walk past that trail or down that trail is for you and you alone to decide.”

I looked down into the paradise bowl and thought about the many things I had learned from my wise old friend. I knew that courage was the key to unlock my dreams and that my fear had spent all its time trying to destroy me. I understood that fear was a clever coward that can only enter the spirit by invitation.

My time with Stikine showed me that courage and action always deliver the same thing. When you live with courage, it makes your soul and spirit free.

The sun grew warmer, and I relaxed and concentrated on my breathing. I looked into my mind, searching for the silence and focus that come only when your thoughts are of nothing. I breathed deeply. I felt like a king grizzly even before I strode down to the marsh flats to meet my old foe.

My time was now. I was where I should have been, living exactly as a grizzly bear should.

I stood, smelled the breeze and looked towards Stikine. “Thank you, my old friend. I have enjoyed our adventures together.”

He stepped closer. "I too have enjoyed our days. I may never see you again, my son, but I wish you courage and strength wherever your journey may take you."

I was confused. I looked deeply into Stikine's eyes, searching for something in him. What stared back wasn't an old, battle-scarred king grizzly anymore—it was me.

Stikine's final words to me are forever etched in my mind. "Rumble, grizzly bear. Rumble."

I turned and started my long, quiet walk down into the marsh flats. My mind was spinning, and with each step I examined my changing thoughts. Soon the stillness was with me again.

I plunged my face into the stream below the hill. I looked up and saw Stikine's golden eagle effortlessly riding the breeze. Beside Nechako, I saw another eagle circling. They seemed to dance, matching each other with every turn, and I hoped that this second eagle was not here to guide me over to the divine.

The hard road can be lonely, but I felt comfort knowing that other great grizzlies had walked this journey before me. Whatever my fate may be, I would face this challenge knowing that all the strength and courage I needed were inside of me, and knowing too that my blood carried a thousand years of great king grizzlies.

As I strode to my destiny, other bears moved away. They could see that today was meant for one thing. Today was for fighting.

When I arrived at the bowl entrance, I paused and looked down at my long black claws. I rolled my neck and loosened my shoulders. My heart beat furiously in my chest, and I concentrated on deep, steady breaths. I pictured Tobaldi before me.

I played out our battle in my mind. Stikine told me to fight with controlled anger, never going too far in one direction or the other. His counsel was to concentrate on a steady progression, conserving energy early on and fighting harder over time. Most bears begin a battle in a state of panic and within seconds, fear saps their power and they become distracted by worries and regrets. Small flesh wounds sting their spirit into thinking that they cannot win the fight.

This battle would be won by the grizzly willing to fight until death stared into his soul.

Now, at the entrance, I paused. "It's just a trail, Rumble. Just a trail."

I took my first step down the well-worn path and was soon enveloped in trees and brush.

"Just a trail, Rumble," I told myself over and over. I felt the grizzly blood stir within me. "Mine. This is mine now," I said.

Ahead the light of the sun began to penetrate the canopy.

"My time. My place. Right now." Quiet anger burned in me. Tobaldi's neck, eyes, ears, and belly. These were my focus.

I stepped boldly into the bowl. A few female grizzlies stood attentively, looking at me closely. As if sensing danger, they quickly trotted away.

I walked carefully now, scoping out the high ground. There, at the rim of the bowl, I saw him.

Tobaldi was lying contentedly beside a sow beneath a great willow. His enormous round face and muzzle had a few more scars since we last met, and silver hair now grew along his back and shoulders.

I noticed a small gravel stretch. The footing looked right. It was where my speed and power would work well. I stalked Tobaldi from downwind.

The huge king of the glen slowly stood, trying to figure out why so many of his females were moving away.

I made it to the gravel pit unnoticed. I was ready.

I stood tall on my hind legs and raised my head to the heavens. I inhaled deeply, and roared my presence to the distant mountains. The sound echoed from the distant cliff-sides, ringing loud and long and fearless and free. I paced at the stone, grinding my teeth.

Tobaldi looked down at me. His initial shock seemed to wither and die, and he began to lope toward me, froth bubbling at his lips. His muscles seemed to swell as his rage boiled over, and in the bright light I could see the slick sheen of his fur. I licked at my fangs and felt my claws sing out for blood.

Tobaldi's head was low and his haunches high. This moment was mine. He was an intruder in my world. I wanted to unleash everything. He would die.

I stood on my back legs, arms at the ready, teeth and fangs gleaming in a sea of froth, taunting Tobaldi onwards.

My foe tore across the grass, growling in anticipation. He lumbered into a full charge, his huge muzzle stretched open, fangs ready to tear and maim.

We met. His enormous bulk slammed into me, and my claws ripped across his face. The momentum sent me rolling backwards, but I landed on my feet and clamped a bite along the back of his neck as we rolled pell-mell through the gravel.

His rage gave him great power, and I was forced to fight with all my strength. Hair was ripped in chunks from my flank as he honed in on my soft underside. I clung onto his back, ripping and tearing at his exposed flesh. I maximize my efforts by inflicting as much pain as I could.

My powerful slashes opened gaping wounds all over his body, but he seemed impervious to pain. He gave no quarter and I sensed that his confidence in his own strength was fueling his frenzy.

Thick gouts of bubbling red poured from a deep gash on the top of my head, but I ignored the hot blood and launched myself back into the fray.

I was not leaving this spot. This was my kingdom now.

I rolled under one of Tobaldi's powerful lunges and used my hind legs to rake my claws across his exposed belly. He roared terribly, smashing a heavy arm across my face. I turned, spitting blood, in time to see a ragged claw swing for my eyes. I ducked, grabbing hold of Tobaldi's snapping face. We threw ourselves forward simultaneously and began to claw at each other's eyes. I lunged, and as my teeth sank deep into Tobaldi's nose, bright red blood gushed out of his nostrils and ran bubbling down his chest.

That's when I heard his first moan of pain.

Incensed, Tobaldi screamed, bearing down on me with his fangs. I believed the battle would never end, but I was not running or giving up. This was my time. He was the intruder. I would take his life as he had tried to take mine.

Tobaldi dropped his shoulders to claw at my chest, but I swallowed the pain and closed in, grabbing his ear between my teeth. I threw all my weight to one side, and Tobaldi slowly corkscrewed down to the gravel. I leapt on top of him. He flattened out, just as Eleven-Thirty had done, and I rained blows along his spine. With every blow, I could actually see the mighty grizzly shake and weaken before me.

It was time to press my advantage. I ripped and slashed at him over and over, and soon he was on the defensive, trying to ward off my blows.

He tried to pull away. I stepped off of him, stood, and roared my challenge. I was strong and ready for even more.

Tobaldi, bleeding badly and breathing in desperate gulps, dragged himself along the gravel. I realized that the fight was over. Tobaldi was a threat no longer, so I let him limp, humbled, into the brush. He did not look back at me.

An eagles scream pulled my mind out of the battle. I stood up and looked off towards the side hill in the distance where my life had been much different only hours ago. Stikine paused and looked back at me one last time as I watched his silhouette crest the ridge. Nechacho dipped and played in the thermals above and soon disappeared from sight.

I was suddenly enormously tired. I had put everything I had into grasping my legacy. The intense pain that washed over me was dulled by the remarkable realization, deep within my *Ursus* spirit, that I had become who I was meant to be: a king grizzly.

I stumbled, bleeding, toward the creek, and slipped into the cooling waters. I let the icy stream wash away the blood and sweat, soothing me. I had won. My thoughts drifted to what my new life would be like in this incredible place. I pulled my head under the churning water and watched the red streams of blood wash quickly away.

The reign of the great Rumble Bear had begun.